Sometimes, wish

Josie was aware that both Cat and Becka were suddenly gazing at her strangely. "What visit?" Becka asked. "Where are you going?"

Josie shrugged. "To meet some family that wants to adopt a kid. Their name's Morgan." She was startled to see Becka go pale.

"Annie and Ben Morgan?" Becka gasped.

"Yeah."

Cat's mouth fell open. "That's who *I'm* going to visit!" she cried.

"Me, too," Becka whispered.

Don't miss these exciting books from HarperPaperbacks!

Collect all the books in the THOROUGHBRED series:

#1 *A Horse Called Wonder*
#2 *Wonder's Promise*
#3 *Wonder's First Race*
#4 *Wonder's Victory*
#5 *Ashleigh's Dream*
#6 *Wonder's Yearling*
#7 *Samantha's Pride*
#8 *Sierra's Steeplechase*
#9 *Pride's Challenge*
#10 *Pride's Last Race**

Also by Joanna Campbell:

Battlecry Forever!
Star of Shadowbrook Farm

And look for:

The Palomino
Christmas Colt
The Forgotten Filly
The Dream Horse

*coming soon

With Friends Like These, Who Needs Enemies?

Marilyn Kaye

HarperPaperbacks

A Division of HarperCollins*Publishers*

For Amy Berkower

This is a work of fiction. The characters, incidents, and dialogues are products of the author's imagination and are not to be construed as real. Any resemblance to actual events or persons, living or dead, is entirely coincidental.

HarperPaperbacks *A Division of* HarperCollins*Publishers*
10 East 53rd Street, New York, N.Y. 10022

Copyright © 1990 by Marilyn Kaye and
Daniel Weiss Associates, Inc.

Cover art copyright © 1993 Daniel Weiss Associates, Inc.

All rights reserved. No part of this book may be used or reproduced in any manner whatsoever without written permission of the publisher, except in the case of brief quotations embodied in critical articles and reviews. For information address Daniel Weiss Associates, Inc., 33 West 17th Street, New York, New York 10011.

Produced by Daniel Weiss Associates, Inc., 33 West 17th Street, New York, New York 10011.

First printing: September 1990

Printed in the United States of America

HarperPaperbacks and colophon are trademarks of HarperCollins*Publishers*

10 9 8 7 6 5 4 3 2

With Friends Like These,
Who Needs Enemies?

One

A shrill bell blasted through the corridors of Willoughby Hall. It was the same bell Cat O'Grady had heard every morning for thirteen years, and it never failed to shatter her dreams. With a moan, she clutched her pillow and pulled it over her head in an attempt to block out the noise.

But as usual, it was impossible. The shrieking alarm wasn't even muffled. Tossing off the pillow, she hoisted herself up on her elbows. As her eyes focused, she made out the figure of a thin girl with long red hair pulling on battered jeans.

When the alarm finally stopped, Cat spoke. "Josie, aren't you going to take a shower?"

"I just took one yesterday."

Cat wrinkled her nose. "You're supposed to take one *every* day."

1

"Says who?" Josie asked. "Is that one of the Ten Commandments? 'Thou shalt take a shower every day'? Gee, I must have missed that one."

Cat sank back on her pillow. Josie was hopeless.

"Besides, I don't have time," Josie continued. "I'm on breakfast duty." Cat watched with unconcealed disgust as Josie proceeded to tuck the T-shirt she'd slept in into her jeans.

Fully dressed, Josie strode across the room, passing the mirror without glancing in it.

"Aren't you even going to comb your hair? It's a rat's nest."

Josie made a face. But she went back to the dresser and grabbed a brush. "Hey, that's mine!" Cat objected.

Josie ignored her and gave her hair one quick swipe, which did little to improve her appearance. "Satisfied?" she asked. Without waiting for an answer, she added, "You better get up if you're planning to spend your usual hour beautifying yourself." She tossed Cat's brush back on the dresser and walked out, twisting her long hair into an untidy braid.

Cat pulled herself up again and looked over to the far end of the room. In the third bed, a fair-haired girl remained blissfully asleep, oblivious to the alarm or the conversation that had been going on.

Cat debated. Should she wake Becka up? If she didn't, Becka would go right on sleeping. She could sleep through an earthquake. She'd be late for roll call, and she'd probably get a demerit.

But then, just two days ago, Becka had forgotten to get Cat for dinner. And Cat had gotten a demerit. It would serve Becka right to get one herself, Cat decided. Trying to make as little noise as possible, Cat got out of bed and tiptoed to where her robe was hanging on its hook.

But Becka must have had her own private inner alarm clock. She stirred, opened her eyes, and sat up. She stared at Cat for a moment. Then, in a small voice, she said, "Oh." That one word resounded with disappointment.

"What's the matter?" Cat asked.

"I was having the most wonderful dream. It was so real."

Cat waited. She didn't have to ask Becka what it was about. She knew Becka would tell her.

"I dreamed that my parents wanted to find me. They were traveling all over the world, running in and out of buildings, searching for me and calling my name."

Cat had heard this one before. "Who were they this time? George Michael and Madonna?"

"I couldn't see their faces. Anyway, just before I woke up, they came to Vermont. And then they were right here, at Willoughby Hall. I could hear them calling." She pulled her knees up and wrapped her arms around them. "You know, they say sometimes dreams can predict the future."

"Oh, Becka, grow up. Look, your parents, or your mother, or somebody, left you on the doorstep right here thirteen years ago. They wouldn't have to go searching for you. They know exactly where you are." Cat didn't think she was being cruel. Becka knew her own history, just like Cat and Josie knew theirs. But unlike Cat and Josie, Becka was a dreamer.

"Okay," Becka conceded. "They wouldn't have to search for me. But the dream could have been telling me they want me back now."

When was she ever going to face reality? Cat wondered. "Becka, if they didn't want you thirteen years ago, why would they suddenly want you now?"

"Maybe they just couldn't keep me when I was born. Maybe they were too poor, or too young, or something. They'd be older now. And maybe they're rich."

"Or maybe they're dead, like my parents and Josie's," Cat countered. "Face facts, Becka. You're an orphan, just like the rest of us. That's why we live in an orphanage. And we're going to go right on being orphans."

"You don't know that for a fact," Becka argued. "We could always be adopted."

Cat snorted. "Sure. Who's going to adopt thirteen-year-old girls when they can have cute little kids or babies?" Tying her robe, she went out into the hall and headed toward the bathroom. Pausing before the bulletin board, she examined the schedule of chores to see what she had to look forward to today. A groan escaped her lips. Laundry. Gross.

The thought of spending a sunny summer morning in the laundry room was depressing. Right now, at this very moment, all her friends from school were off at summer camp or on vacation with their families. They were lying on beaches, playing tennis, and just generally having fun. A wave of self-pity engulfed Cat. She was probably the only thirteen-year-old girl in the world who'd be spending the day doing laundry.

Continuing down the hall, she could hear the usual commotion coming from one of the big rooms, where eight younger girls slept. The high-pitched giggles and chatter reminded her of one benefit to being one of the three oldest girls at Willoughby Hall. They got their own room instead of having to sleep in a ward. They got allowances, too—not big ones, but enough for an occasional bottle of nail polish or a lipstick. Of course, there were drawbacks to being the oldest, too. Like having more chores than anyone else.

Luckily there was an empty shower stall in the big bathroom, and Cat didn't have to wait. She showered quickly and put her robe back on. Hurrying out, she practically collided with a girl on her way in.

"Hey, look where you're going!" Cat said.

Cat waited for an apology. She usually got respect from the younger kids. But this girl just shrugged. Cat eyed her curiously and realized she'd never seen her before. "Who are you?"

The slight girl, who looked to be about ten, raised

sullen eyes. "Trixie," she mumbled. She brushed past Cat and went into one of the stalls.

Cat wasn't offended by her rudeness. New kids were like that sometimes, still in a state of shock at suddenly finding themselves in an orphanage. She'll adjust, Cat thought. The bells, the inspections, the pukey green color of the halls and rooms, and the noise created by over thirty boys and girls—she'd get used to it eventually.

She pushed Trixie from her mind. She had her own problems—like how she was going to get herself pulled together in fifteen minutes.

Back in her room, she went to the dresser and pulled out her prize possession—a pair of designer jeans that had unexpectedly shown up in a donation box. Then she put on a T-shirt and went to the mirror. Behind her, Becka was still curled up on her bed, her face buried in a book. "You better start getting dressed," Cat warned her.

Becka didn't even look up. "Mmm." Cat shook her head wearily. Once Becka opened a book, she was dead to the world.

Cat leaned closer to the mirror and began stroking green shadow over her eyelids. She added a matching green eyeliner, extending the line just beyond her eyes like the girl at the makeup counter had shown her. Then she stepped back to examine the effect.

The salesgirl was right. The color did enhance her eyes. Not that they needed much enhancing. Cat's brilliant emerald green eyes were definitely her best feature.

But her hair ran a close second. Thick, glossy, black waves framed her heart-shaped face and drifted down to her shoulders. A regular colleen, Mrs. Parker, the cook, had once called her. Cat liked that. Even though she'd never set foot in Ireland, it was nice knowing that her parents' birthplace was reflected in her appearance. Sometimes she wondered if she looked like either of them. All she had been told was that they'd died in a boating accident, shortly after coming to the United States. She didn't even have a photo of them.

She tossed her head, turned to a three-quarter profile, and gave herself a sidelong look. Nice pose. She was glad Josie wasn't there, and Becka was too absorbed in her reading to notice her performance. They were always teasing her about how conceited she was. She always denied it, pointing out her knobby knees and her nose, which, in her opinion, turned up way too much.

But in the privacy of her own thoughts, she didn't have to be so modest. She was pretty and she knew it. And maybe someday, when she was rich, she could have her nose fixed. She might even be beautiful then.

Oh, Cat, you are conceited, she thought, almost laughing out loud at her own vanity. Quickly, she covered her mouth, which she considered another flaw. It was too wide.

The door swung open, and Josie tore in. "Funny, somehow I knew I'd find you in that position."

"What do you mean?" Cat asked.

"In front of the mirror, admiring yourself."

"You could do with an occasional look in the mirror yourself," Cat retorted. "What are you doing back here, anyway? I thought you were on breakfast duty in the kitchen."

"I spilled orange juice on my shirt."

Cat gave her a look of exaggerated surprise. "Josie Taylor spilled something on herself? How unusual!" She looked pointedly at Josie's shirt, which already contained a wide variety of stains.

"Very funny," Josie growled. She opened a drawer and pulled out another shirt, only slightly less stained than the one she had on. "Hey, Becka, you've got five minutes."

"Mmm."

Josie took off one shirt and put on the other. Then she marched over to Becka's bed and snatched the book from her hands.

"Hey!" Becka cried in outrage.

"Didn't you hear me? It's five minutes till roll call!"

Becka looked down at her nightgown, suddenly aware of the fact that she wasn't dressed. "Ohmigosh!" She jumped up and ran to the closet.

Josie examined the book Becka had been reading. *"Jane Eyre,"* she said, pronouncing the second word "ire."

8

"It's pronounced 'air,'" Becka said, her voice muffled by the shirt she was pulling over her head. *"Jane Eyre."*

"I thought you read that before," Cat murmured as she applied blush liberally to her cheeks.

Becka was tying a long, flowered wraparound skirt around her waist. "This is the third time I've read it. Or maybe it's the fourth."

Cat picked up her brush and eyed with distaste the strands of red hair Josie had left in it. She picked them out. "Why do you want to read the same book over and over?"

"Because it's good. It's about an orphan."

"Surprise, surprise," Cat said. Becka was always reading books about pitiful orphans. Personally, Cat preferred a good teen romance.

Josie tossed the book back on Becka's bed. "And I'll bet she gets adopted by a big family and lives happily ever after."

"No, she doesn't," Becka replied. "She lives with this horrible, mean aunt who sends her to an orphanage. The orphanage is really awful. They have to eat cold porridge."

"She should have gone to Willoughby Hall," Josie said. "We're having pancakes today."

"There's a happy ending," Becka went on. "She leaves the orphanage and becomes a governess. Then she falls in love with this mysterious man, and they're going to get married, only she finds out he has this terrible secret and runs away. But they get back together in the end."

"I don't get it," Cat said. She bent over to brush her hair from the back to give it more body. "What good is reading a book when you already know how it's going to end?"

"But that's what makes it so nice," Becka said, taking Cat's place at the mirror. She made a futile attempt to flatten her frizzy hair. "I can cry at the beginning, when Jane suffers. But I know everything's going to be okay for her, so I don't get *too* upset."

"That's weird," Josie stated. "How can you cry over someone in a story? She's not even real."

Becka gave up on her hair. "Maybe if you read a book once in a while you'd understand."

"No, thanks," Josie said. "I'd rather *do* things. Not sit around reading about them. Hey, Cat!"

On her way to the door, Cat turned. "What?"

"You've got the most horrible stain right on the seat of your jeans!"

Cat gasped. She hurried to the mirror and stood with her back to it, twisting her head to see her reflection. But the mirror wasn't long enough. She ran to the little desk in the corner, grabbed the chair, and dragged it across the room. Placing it in front of the mirror, she climbed onto it.

Then she realized Becka was giggling. And Josie was practically doubled over.

Cat stood there on the chair and gazed at them coldly. "There's no stain on my pants, is there?"

Still laughing, Josie ambled out of the room. Cat kept her eyes fixed on Becka. She knew a really long, intense glare would scare her. Sure enough, Becka's smile faded and she bit her lower lip. Then she fled.

From her position on the chair, Cat could turn and see her whole back. As she'd suspected, there was nothing on the seat of her jeans. After so many years with those two, she should have known better.

With a deep, aggravated sigh, she leaped off the chair and ran out of the room.

Two

On the main floor, just outside the dining hall, Josie took her place in the long line of kids. Becka fell in right beside her. They had made it in the nick of time. Karen, one of the counselors, had started calling roll and was just getting to the B's.

"Becka Blue?"

There was no response.

"Becka Blue?"

Josie poked her. "Here," Becka gasped, still out of breath from her dash down the two flights.

Mrs. Scanlon emerged from her office. The director of Willoughby Hall always conducted the morning inspection herself. She started at the end of the line farthest from Josie.

Out of the corner of her eye, Josie could see Cat racing down the stairs. Would she make it into the line before Mrs. Scanlon spotted her? Josie's eyes shifted to the tall, elegant-looking director. She was talking to a counselor and she had her back to the stairway. Running on tiptoes, Cat slid into place next to Josie.

Josie felt a mild twinge of disappointment. She wouldn't have minded seeing Cat get into a little trouble. Nothing major—just a frown and a lecture on tardiness, something to bring her down a notch. Cat was so high-and-mighty sometimes, such a know-it-all. She was so full of herself, she could really get on Josie's nerves. And she did, frequently. The thought of Mrs. Scanlon scolding Cat right here in front of everyone wasn't exactly an unpleasant image.

But Josie knew it wouldn't happen. Cat hardly ever got into trouble. Not that she was some goody-goody who never did anything wrong. But somehow she always managed to avoid being caught.

"Catherine O'Grady?" the counselor called.

"Here," Cat replied. As soon as the counselor's eyes were off her, she gave Josie a sidelong look. "No thanks to *you*," she hissed.

Josie kept her eyes forward. At least she had the satisfaction of knowing Cat had gotten one demerit that week—and Josie could take the credit for it. A couple of days ago, Becka had been on her way to get Cat for dinner. Josie had managed to distract Becka long enough to make Cat late.

"Josie Taylor?"

"Here." She could see Mrs. Scanlon getting

closer. Right now, she was speaking to a boy just a few feet away. "Oh, dear, look at your fingernails." Her tone was gentle. Mrs. Scanlon never yelled. But for some reason the way she scolded a person made them feel worse than if she'd thrown a fit.

Josie glanced down at her own fingernails. They didn't look so great either. Of course, they weren't dirty. Mrs. Parker would never let her work in the kitchen with dirty hands or fingernails. But they *were* kind of chewed-up.

Mrs. Scanlon passed Becka with a smile and a nod. She didn't comment on what Josie considered to be Becka's weird getup. Becka never wore anything normal, like jeans. Today she had on a dumb-looking long skirt and a blouse with faded lace.

When the donation boxes came, Becka always grabbed the most peculiar stuff, like a feather boa or a torn silk shawl with fringe. Josie figured Mrs. Scanlon was probably so used to Becka's crazy costumes that she didn't even pay attention to them anymore.

She braced herself for her own inspection. Mrs. Scanlon's smile faded slightly as they stood face to face. But she spoke softly. "Josie, your hair . . ."

Josie's hand flew up to her unruly braid. "I guess I forgot to brush it."

Mrs. Scanlon put her hand lightly on Josie's arm. "Try to remember from now on."

"Yes, ma'am." She sneaked a peek at Cat. Cat's face revealed nothing, but Josie felt pretty sure she was snickering inside.

14

But at least Cat didn't pass inspection without a comment. Mrs. Scanlon looked at her reprovingly. "Now Cat, I don't think all that eye makeup is necessary. As soon as breakfast is over, I want you to wash it off."

Even though Cat responded politely, Josie knew she was seething inside. And as soon as they were dismissed to go into the dining hall, she started complaining. "Honestly, you'd think makeup was a sin or something."

"It ain't sinful," Josie replied, "just stupid."

"Don't say ain't," Becka said. "It's bad grammar."

Josie knew that. She just used words like *ain't* to annoy people.

"I wouldn't expect you to understand about makeup," Cat said. "You're too immature." Josie didn't bother with a comeback for that. It was one of Cat's standard insults, not worth responding to.

In the dining hall, Josie took her place behind the counter with Mrs. Parker as the residents lined up for breakfast. She took a plate from the stack and held it out. Mrs. Parker flipped pancakes from the griddle onto the plate. Josie added bacon and orange slices, put the plate on a tray, and handed it to the first kid in line.

"Smells great," Josie said.

"That's because you did such a good job mixing the batter," Mrs. Parker replied.

Josie grinned at the plump, gray-haired cook. If there was anyone she loved in the world, it was Mrs.

15

Parker. She was the only person at Willoughby Hall who never criticized her.

"How was inspection?" Mrs. Parker asked.

"Not great. I didn't brush my hair. But what's the point? Even when I do brush it, it sticks out."

Mrs. Parker gave her an appraising look as she flipped pancakes onto another plate. "That's because it's so thick. Maybe you should get it cut very short."

Josie considered that. "Hey, that's a good idea. If I didn't have a lot of hair, I wouldn't have to spend so much time taking care of it."

"I'll speak to Mrs. Scanlon. Maybe when I go grocery shopping this week, you can come along and we'll stop at the beauty parlor."

Josie couldn't think of anything more enjoyable than spending a day shopping with Mrs. Parker. "But I don't need a beauty parlor," Josie told her. "A barber will do. I could get it cut really short, like a boy." As she handed over a tray, she noticed that Becka was next in line, with Cat right behind her.

"Pancakes, mmm," Becka sighed. "Josie, can I have an extra one?"

"Three per person," Josie replied.

"I'll just take two pancakes," Cat said. "She can have my third."

Josie didn't blame Becka for looking startled by Cat's generosity. It certainly wasn't typical of her.

"Gee, thanks," Becka said.

Cat smiled. "I'm watching my figure." She looked

pointedly at Becka's slightly protruding stomach. "Some of us care about how we look."

As the meaning behind Cat's words penetrated, Josie watched Becka's face fall. She lowered her head and started twisting a lock of her hair. "Here," Josie said, thrusting a plate with four pancakes at her. Then she got a plate for Cat and turned to Mrs. Parker. "Just two for Cat. Got any burned ones?"

"Now, Josie." Mrs. Parker slid two pancakes onto the plate. Handing it to Cat, Josie glared, but Cat wasn't looking. When she turned away, Josie made a face. Cat was always cutting them down, making cracks about their hair, their clothes, all those silly things. It didn't bother Josie, but it always got to Becka. *Becka shouldn't care so much about how she looks,* Josie thought. *Then Cat's insults wouldn't hurt her.*

"Why do girls act so goofy?" she wondered. She didn't realize she'd spoken out loud until she noticed that Mrs. Parker was smiling in amusement.

"And what do you think you are?" the cook asked.

Josie amended her opinion. "Some girls. They're always fussing about how they look, whether they're too fat or too thin, and putting on all that gooky makeup."

"You say that now," Mrs. Parker said. "But I'll bet you'll change your tune in a very short time."

Josie held out another plate. "Why would I do that?"

"It's only natural," Mrs. Parker said. "Girls start

thinking about their hair and their figure and their looks when they start thinking about boys."

"That's dumb. I'll never think about boys. At least, not *that* way."

"Oh, I don't believe that," Mrs. Parker said. "You'll want to have dates someday. And you'll want to get married and have a family."

"Never," Josie said firmly. "All I want are horses."

Mrs. Parker smiled fondly at her. "You could have a husband, a family, and a horse, too."

Josie shook her head. "I don't just want a horse to ride once in a while. When I grow up, I'm gonna be surrounded by horses. I'll be a horse trainer, or maybe I'll join a rodeo. If I don't get too tall, I could even be a jockey."

"You have to be a pretty fine rider to do those things," Mrs. Parker reminded her.

"I know." Josie was silent for a moment. "I wish I could take riding lessons."

"Well, maybe, someday . . ."

"Not any time soon," Josie sighed. "Not while I'm at Willoughby Hall. The last time I was on a horse was when a counselor took a bunch of us to the county fair. That must have been two years ago."

"Was that your only time on a horse?"

"No." A vague memory formed in her mind. It was an image of herself as a tiny child sitting on a horse. She wasn't alone. A big man sat behind her

18

with one hand on the reins and the other around her waist, holding her. . . .

The vision was shattered by a plaintive voice. "Hey! I'm hungry!"

"Okay, okay." Josie handed the tray to the boy on the other side of the counter.

"Well, I've heard of girls being horse crazy," Mrs. Parker said, "but you take the cake."

"That's because I'm from Texas," Josie reminded her. "All Texans are horse crazy."

"But you left Texas when you were only five years old."

Josie lifted her head proudly. "You can take a girl out of Texas, but you can't take Texas out of the girl." She handed a tray to the last person in line and fixed one for herself. "See you at lunchtime!"

Grabbing silverware and a napkin from the end of the counter, she carried her tray to her regular seat between Cat and Becka at one of the long tables. Across from them sat the new girl. Josie couldn't remember her name. "Hi," she said to her. The girl didn't respond. She was mashing her pancakes with her fork.

At the front of the room, Mrs. Scanlon rose from her table. "Good morning, boys and girls. Could I have everyone's attention for an announcement?"

"I wonder what would happen if we all said no," Josie whispered. She could have sworn she saw a flicker of a smile on the new girl's face.

"I want you all to meet a new counselor," Mrs.

Scanlon continued. "This is Ellen Perry. Ellen, would you like to say a few words?"

A slender, smiling girl with long, straight, brown hair stood up. "I'd just like to say that I'm really happy to be working here. I'm looking forward to getting to know each and every one of you. And I'm counting on all of you to help me out. I just graduated from college with a degree in social work, and this is my first real job."

Looking out over the room, Josie could see some kids exchange knowing grins. A new counselor was fair game for any prank they could get away with. Josie wasn't grinning. "A social worker. Double yuck." She'd known a ton of them already. She'd just as soon not know another.

Becka paused between bites of pancakes. "I think she looks nice, like she'd be easy to talk to. I want to get to know her."

"Why?" Josie asked. "She won't stay long." She noticed a puzzled expression on the face of the girl across the table, so she explained. "These counselors come and go. I guess being around thirty orphans is too much for them."

"She's right," Cat said to the new girl. "And I'll give you some free advice. Don't ever get too attached to a counselor. Becka's always doing that, and then she goes berserk when they leave."

"I do not!" Becka exclaimed indignantly.

"Oh no? Remember Lauren?" Cat turned to the

20

new girl. "She only cried herself to sleep for a week when Lauren left."

That was true, but Josie thought it was mean of Cat to tell the new girl.

"I wouldn't cry over just any counselor," Becka said. "Lauren was special. She used to lend me books. And we'd talk about them." She turned to Josie. "I'll bet you'd cry if Mrs. Parker left."

"I *never* cry." But the mere thought of being separated from Mrs. Parker was unnerving. How *would* she feel if Mrs. Parker wasn't around? Pretty awful, she guessed. But she wouldn't cry.

Suddenly she wanted to change the subject. "You're new here, right?"

The girl gave a slight nod.

"What's your name?"

"Trixie."

"I'm Josie Taylor. This is Becka Blue. And that's—"

"We already met," Cat interrupted.

Trixie cocked her head to one side. "Becka *Blue?* That's a weird last name."

"It's not my real name. Actually, nobody knows what my real last name is. I was found on the doorstep of Willoughby Hall when I was just a few days old. There was a note pinned to my blanket, but all it said was 'Becka.' The blanket was blue, so they called me Becka Blue."

"How old are you?"

"Thirteen." Becka indicated the others beside her. "We're all thirteen."

"You mean you've been here for thirteen years?" There was no mistaking the horror in Trixie's voice.

Josie felt an immediate urge to defend Willoughby Hall. "Hey, there are worse places. I know. I've been in them."

Trixie didn't look convinced, so Josie continued. "My parents died when I was five. They were killed in a car accident."

Trixie just stared at her. Josie figured she was probably wondering how anyone could talk about such a tragedy like that, so casually and matter-of-factly. If only she knew how much effort it took, how hard Josie had practiced to be able to talk about her parents without showing emotion. She knew from experience that all it took was a slight tremble in her voice, the tiniest tear forming in her eye, to make people pity her. And pity was not something she wanted from anyone.

"Anyway, after they died, I was sent to live with this cousin of my father's here in Vermont. But she had her own kids, and she didn't really want me."

"How could you tell?" Trixie asked.

Josie shrugged. "I just could. Besides, she dumped me after about six months."

Trixie's eyes were wide. "Where did you go then?"

"I was put in a foster home."

"What was that like?" Trixie asked.

The memory made Josie shudder, but she forced her voice to sound nonchalant. "It stunk. This woman, she used to hit me. I told the social worker who visited, but she didn't believe me until I showed her my black-and-blue marks."

Trixie gasped. Hastily, before Trixie could say anything, Josie continued. "Then I was sent to another foster home. They didn't hit me there, but they basically ignored me. I think they only kept me for the money the state paid them. I guess they didn't take very good care of me, or maybe they just got sick of me. All I know is the social worker showed up one day, and the next thing I knew, I was here."

Cat was getting annoyed that she wasn't the center of this new girl's attention. She broke into the conversation. "My parents drowned. They were from Ireland, and no one could find any relatives. They probably didn't look very hard." She paused dramatically. "Someday, I'm going to Ireland to find my family."

"But like I was saying," Josie interrupted, "they treat you okay here. Mrs. Scanlon's nice, and the food's good."

"Do kids ever get adopted?" Trixie asked.

"Oh, sure," Becka said. Her voice became wistful. "The babies do, of course. And sometimes the little ones. But no one's interested in older kids like us."

"Better face it," Cat said. "You're stuck here, just like us."

"No, I'm not," Trixie said.

23

Cat raised her eyebrows. "You think you're going to be adopted?"

"I don't need to be adopted," Trixie said. "I've already got parents."

The three older girls exchanged looks. This was a typical remark from someone new. They weren't ready to admit they were really orphans.

Trixie was watching their expressions and she scowled. "I do so have parents."

Cat sniffed. "Oh yeah? Then where are they? What are you doing here in an orphanage?"

Trixie pushed her chair away from the table. "I gotta go." She jumped up and ran out of the dining hall.

"Poor girl," Becka said.

Josie disliked showing sympathy almost as much as she hated receiving it. "Don't worry about her. She's just going to have to face the fact that she has no family."

"And that she's stuck here at Willoughby Hall like the rest of us," Cat added.

"You make it sound like a jail," Josie said. "It's not so bad here. And being the oldest, we get lots of privileges."

"We get first crack at the donation boxes," Becka reminded Cat.

Cat's upper lip curled. "Secondhand clothes. Goody goody."

"And we get to go places," Becka said. "As long

as you ask permission a day in advance, Mrs. Scanlon's good about saying yes."

That didn't impress Cat. "Other kids get to go wherever they want whenever they want."

"Well, we're not other kids," Josie said.

Cat grimaced. "You can say that again."

Josie complied. "We're not other kids."

"Oh, shut up," Cat muttered. Sullenly, she picked at her orange slices.

"Hello, girls." Josie looked up. The new counselor, Ellen Something, was standing there.

Cat's expression was transformed. She smiled at the girl brightly. "Hi! I'm Cat O'Grady."

Becka turned an eager expression to the counselor. "My name is Becka Blue."

Josie took her time chewing a bite of bacon. Finally, she said, "Josie Taylor."

"I particularly wanted to meet you three," Ellen said. "Mrs. Scanlon told me you're the oldest ones here. I hope we can be friends."

"That would be great," Cat said. "By the way, I *love* your dress."

Josie concentrated on what was left of her breakfast. Cat was always kissing up to counselors, because she knew it was the easiest way to get special privileges.

Becka was gushing over the new counselor, too, but for different reasons. She was always looking for some affection.

Both of them made Josie uncomfortable. But it

was Cat who made her feel sick. At least Becka was sincere. Cat was such a total phony.

Like she'd told Trixie, there were worse places to be than Willoughby Hall. But she couldn't imagine a worse roommate than Cat O'Grady.

Three

Becka drained the last of her orange juice and got up.

"What are you in such a hurry to get to?" Josie asked.

"I'm on nursery duty."

"Ugh," Cat commented. "That's even worse than laundry. Listening to babies screaming, changing diapers . . ." She wrinkled her nose.

Becka had heard Cat say this before, but she still found it hard to believe. How could anyone prefer folding sheets to working in the nursery? Becka didn't even mind changing diapers. There was always the pleasure afterward of cuddling a freshly powdered, sweet-smelling infant.

Josie didn't share Becka's enthusiasm either. "I'm glad I got out of taking care of babies."

"That's because you dropped one last month," Becka reminded her. "Lucky for him, he landed on his rear end instead of his head. I'm surprised Mrs. Parker lets you work in the kitchen. The floor must be covered with broken eggs."

"I don't drop eggs," Josie replied. "Just babies."

Cat started laughing. Becka was apalled. How could they even think that was funny? Shaking her head, she brought her tray up to the conveyor belt and hurried out of the dining hall.

The nursery was down at the other end of the corridor. It was Becka's favorite room at Willoughby Hall. All the other rooms had a boring sameness—green walls, overhead lights that were too bright, dull, plain furniture. But the nursery was different. Last year, two counselors had painted it pale blue and covered one wall with a huge multicolored rainbow. They'd stenciled clowns and teddy bears on another wall. There were brightly striped curtains and mobiles hanging over the cribs. In the corner sat a big, cozy rocking chair.

"I'm here," Becka announced to Linda, the counselor who was sitting in the chair just inside the nursery. Linda put a finger to her lips. "They're sleeping." She got up. "I'll be back in an hour," she whispered.

Becka peered into each of the four occupied cribs. When she reached the last one, she paused and smiled. This particular little girl, still without a name, was her very favorite. She was the smallest of the bunch, and Becka thought she was the sweetest. Even in sleep her lips were curled into a smile. Becka reached down and lightly stroked the soft blond fuzz on her head.

"I wonder what your name will be," she said in a whisper. "I wish I could name you. You should have a special, beautiful name. Like Clarissa. No . . . Aurora! That's what I'll call you. It's Sleeping Beauty's real name. Someday I'll read you that story if you're still here."

She was glad no one could see her right now. How Josie and Cat would laugh if they heard her talking to sleeping babies! They could never understand how special babies were to her. Every time she looked at them, especially this one, she saw herself. She saw a bundle on the doorstep, a blue blanket wrapped around a helpless, fragile baby Becka. Unwanted and unloved, just like these babies.

How could anyone give up a baby? she wondered. No matter how poor she was, or how alone and frightened, she couldn't imagine giving away her own child. *Why didn't your mother and father want you?* she asked Aurora silently. Of course, what she really wanted to know was why her own parents hadn't wanted her. She wasn't at all surprised to feel tears forming in her eyes.

She quickly brushed them away. It was annoying how easily she cried. The others were always making fun of her for it. All it took was a sad song, or movie, or book, or even a dumb TV show to turn her into a walking sprinkler system.

She wished she could be brave and strong like Josie. Josie was amazing the way she could talk about her parents being killed in an accident without showing even the slightest sign of grief.

And Cat. Cat didn't seem to care one bit that she couldn't remember her parents. Becka could never be like that, cold and unfeeling. But she wouldn't mind having some of Cat's confidence. She was so sure of herself. At school no one ever thought of Cat as one of the poor, pathetic orphans.

Sometimes Becka wished she could be anyone but herself. Maybe that was why she liked reading so much, particularly books about girls doing exciting and amazing things. She could imagine herself as a princess living a glamorous life in a castle. Or a pilot flying a plane across the ocean all by herself.

But these were just crazy fantasies. She didn't have much chance of becoming a princess. And in all honesty she had to admit the thought of flying a plane made her stomach turn over.

Then, like a lightning flash, she had a brilliant idea. She could be an actress! She could play roles and be anything she wanted to be—a queen, an astronaut, a gypsy . . . As her mind reeled with the possibilities, little Aurora opened her eyes. A split second later, she opened her mouth.

Becka gently lifted her up before her wails could wake the other babies. "What's the matter, Aurora?" she asked. Fortunately, Aurora didn't have to tell her. A quick feel of her diaper provided the answer.

Becka carried her over to the changing table. As she went about changing Aurora's diaper, her thoughts went back to her new ambition. Why hadn't she ever thought about becoming an actress before? It was the perfect job for her. She immediately discarded all her previous plans for her future: teacher, writer, artist. Those were just whims. An actress was what she was meant to be.

As she reached for the baby powder, she caught sight of her reflection in the mirror above the table. Did an actress have to be beautiful? Becka tried to be objective as she studied her frizzy hair, her pug nose, that front tooth that slightly overlapped the one next to it.

Well, the tooth could be fixed. And maybe, if she could get a decent cut, her hair would be okay. Or she could wear a wig.

As for her height—or lack of it—there was still the possibility she might grow a few inches. That left her figure. She sighed. For the zillionth time she vowed to go on a diet.

She powdered Aurora and the baby's cries were reduced to whimpers. Then she put a clean diaper on her and carried her to the chair. Humming softly, she rocked the baby in her arms.

Of course, good looks weren't all an actress needed. She had to have talent, too. "Do you think I have talent?" Becka asked Aurora. The baby smiled and made cooing sounds. Something about this struck a chord. . . .

31

Oh, right, that movie she'd seen on TV a few nights earlier. It was about a woman who had adopted a baby boy, but then the birth mother changed her mind and wanted him back. Becka remembered the scene when the social worker came to take the baby away from the woman who had adopted him. It was so dramatic. The actress had been sitting just like Becka was now, in a rocking chair with the baby in her arms.

Becka raised her head and imagined the social worker standing at the door. She hugged the baby tighter to her chest. "No! You can't have him! He's mine!" She stood up and faced the invisible social worker with an anguished expression.

"Please, let me keep him," she pleaded. "I can give him a much better home than his wretched mother." She lowered her head and gazed adoringly at the infant. "I love him. And I won't let you take him away!"

"Becka, what are you doing?"

Becka looked up. A real person was standing in the doorway—and it wasn't a television social worker. Mrs. Scanlon had her hands on her hips and a perplexed expression on her face.

"I, uh, was just talking to Aurora."

"To whom?"

"I mean, this baby." Becka gave Mrs. Scanlon an abashed smile. "I named her Aurora. Don't you think that's pretty?"

Mrs. Scanlon smiled back, but her eyes reflected

concern. "Yes, it's a very pretty name. But I think we should leave that privilege to her parents, don't you?"

Becka bit her lip. "Has she been adopted?"

"Yes. Her new parents will be coming for her in a few days."

"Oh." Aurora—or whatever her name would be —had fallen asleep. Becka carried her back to the crib and laid her down. Mrs. Scanlon came up behind her.

"Becka, you know you shouldn't get too attached to the babies. They never stay here very long."

"I know," Becka murmured. Babies came and went faster than counselors. "Mrs. Scanlon, how come I wasn't adopted when I was a baby?"

"That's hard to say, Becka. There were more babies available back then and fewer people seeking to adopt. And you have to realize that often adoptive parents are very particular about a baby's background. They want to know everything about the birth parents —their health, intelligence, that sort of thing. There was nothing we could tell them about you."

Becka couldn't think of anything to say. She felt that familiar stinging in her eyes. Mrs. Scanlon placed a hand on her shoulder. "You haven't been so miserable here at Willoughby Hall, have you, Becka?"

"Oh, no," Becka assured her. "It's just that . . . well, sometimes I wonder what it would be like to have a real family. And now it's too late for me. I'm too old."

"That's not true. In fact, that's what I've come to talk to you about. There's a very nice couple who is interested in adopting. And they're looking for an older child.''

Becka's head jerked up. Had she heard correctly? ''Who are they?''

''Their names are Annie and Ben Morgan, and they're in their early forties. They never had any children of their own because they were so busy with careers in New York. Now that they've settled here in Vermont, they want to make a real home for themselves.''

''But why do they want an older child?''

''Well, they want a family, but they feel they're too old to start with a new baby.''

Becka swallowed. ''And . . . and you think they might want to adopt *me*?''

''Now, I don't want you to get your hopes up,'' Mrs. Scanlon cautioned. ''I've told them about you, and they'd like to meet you. In fact, they've invited you to come visit for a couple of days.''

As Becka absorbed this news, she could feel her heart quicken. Her expression must have given away her feelings, because Mrs. Scanlon became very serious. ''Becka, I don't want you to be disappointed if this doesn't work out. It's not just a question of whether or not the Morgans want you. Remember, it's your decision, too. After all, you might not want to be adopted by the Morgans. Becka? Are you listening to me?''

Becka was too dazed to speak. All she could do was nod her head.

"And you'd like to visit the Morgans?"

Becka managed to squeak out, "Yes, ma'am."

"Then I'll call them now."

In the large kitchen, Josie was making sandwiches for lunch. She knew the routine by heart. On the big worktable, she had already laid out twenty slices of bread. She began placing two slices of bologna on each. When that was finished, she topped them with cheese slices. The lettuce and tomato wouldn't be added until just before lunchtime, to keep the sandwiches from getting soggy. Twenty slices of bread— ten sandwiches. Josie did it three times. Over by the stove, Mrs. Parker was adding carrots to a huge vat of vegetable soup.

"What are we making for dinner tonight?" Josie asked the cook. Mrs. Parker left the stove and went to the refrigerator. Opening it, she stood there for a moment and surveyed the contents.

"Chicken," she decided. "How about whipping up some of that fancy barbecue sauce of yours? We could put the chicken in to marinate now."

"Okay," Josie agreed. "Have we got all the ingredients?"

From the refrigerator, Mrs. Parker pulled out a bag of tomatoes, some green peppers, and onions. Josie went to a cabinet and found tomato paste and olive oil. She assembled them on the counter with the vegetables. "What about fresh garlic?"

Mrs. Parker went back to the refrigerator and

poked around. Then she tossed Josie a clove. "Don't be too generous with that. The last time you made your sauce it took me a week to get the smell out of this kitchen."

Josie laughed at the exaggeration. "Come on, Mrs. Parker, you know you can't make a good barbecue sauce without plenty of garlic."

"Just don't go overboard, okay?"

Josie took a sharp knife and went to work chopping the peppers into tiny bits. She'd almost finished when the knife slipped. "Ow!"

"Good grief, child." Mrs. Parker wiped her hands on her apron and hurried over. "What kind of damage have you done to yourself now?"

Josie sucked on her finger. "It's just a tiny cut. No big deal."

"Let me see," Mrs. Parker demanded. Josie held out the injured finger. Mrs. Parker examined the wound closely.

"It's just a surface cut this time," she said in relief. "As I recall, the last time you went clear through to the bone." She practically dragged Josie to the sink, turned on the faucet, and ran water over the cut. Then she swabbed it with some antiseptic. Josie gritted her teeth at the familiar sting.

"Has there ever been a time when you weren't wearing a bandage of some sort?" Mrs. Parker asked as she put an adhesive strip over the cut.

"Either that or a cast. They know me by name in

the hospital emergency room. I guess I'm just accident-prone."

"Don't make jokes about it," Mrs. Parker warned her. "You've got to be more careful. One of these days you could really hurt yourself."

"Nah. I'm tough."

"I wonder. I've got a feeling you're not anywhere near as tough as you'd like to think you are."

Josie struck a mock-threatening pose. "Wanna bet?"

"You just get back to work, young lady."

In comfortable silence, Mrs. Parker returned to her soup and Josie started preparing her sauce. Somehow she managed to get the rest of the ingredients chopped up without any more accidents. She dumped everything into a pot on the stove, turned on the flame, and stirred.

Mrs. Parker leaned over the pot and sniffed appreciatively. "You know, Josie, for someone who's not into feminine things, you certainly have a knack for cooking."

"You don't have to be female to be a good cook," Josie retorted. "Did you know that some of the best chefs in the world are men?" She dipped a spoon into her sauce and tasted it. "This needs something." She searched through a cabinet and found some hot pepper sauce.

"Go easy on that," Mrs. Parker ordered her.

"A good barbecue sauce needs some kick to it," Josie argued. "That's the Texas style."

"Well, the rest of us don't have Texas tastebuds," Mrs. Parker replied. She watched closely as Josie tossed a few drops of the pepper sauce into the pot. "That's enough!"

Reluctantly, Josie put the bottle aside, but she kept it within easy reach so she could sneak in a few more drops when the cook wasn't looking.

"Goodness, something certainly smells delicious in here, Mrs. Parker."

Josie turned to see Mrs. Scanlon standing in the doorway. Mrs. Parker beamed. "I can't take the credit for it. You can thank our Josie. She's making us her special sauce for tonight's chicken. Is there something I can get you, Mrs. Scanlon?"

"No, I just wanted a word with Josie."

Uh-oh, Josie thought. *What did I do now?* She watched Mrs. Scanlon's face uneasily.

"Josie, would you be interested in going to visit a family for a couple of days? They live on a small farm about an hour from here."

Josie grimaced. "Is this one of those do-good families who want to treat a poor pitiful orphan to some fresh air?"

Mrs. Scanlon raised her eyebrows at this sarcasm.

"Sorry," Josie said quickly. "But why do I have to go visit this family?"

"You don't *have* to visit them," said Mrs. Scanlon. "Their names are Annie and Ben Morgan, and they're interested in adopting." Abruptly, Josie turned away and began stirring her sauce. Mrs. Scanlon continued. "They're looking for an older girl. Now you certainly don't have to go if you don't want to. But I think it could be a pleasant experience for you. Josie, please look at me when I'm speaking to you."

Josie turned back and faced her.

"Would you like to visit the Morgans?"

For a moment Josie was silent. "You said they live on a farm?"

"That's right."

"Is it a horse farm?" she asked hopefully.

"Actually, I do remember Mrs. Morgan saying something about a horse."

Josie thought for another minute. "Okay," she said finally. "I'll go."

"Good. I'll make the arrangements." With that, Mrs. Scanlon left the kitchen.

"Well!" Mrs. Parker exclaimed. "How about that?"

"Should I start washing the lettuce now?" Josie asked. When Mrs. Parker didn't reply, she asked, "Why are you looking at me like that?"

"I'm a little puzzled."

"About what?"

"About you. I thought you'd be excited. You don't even seem particularly interested. These people are looking to adopt an older child. How many opportunities come around like that?"

Josie shrugged. "I don't know."

"Wouldn't you like to be adopted? Live in a home, with a family who loves you?"

"I don't know." She was beginning to sound like a broken record.

Suddenly, the puzzlement in Mrs. Parker's eyes was replaced by understanding. "Oh, Josie. You're frightened, aren't you?"

Josie stiffened. "Why should I be frightened?"

Mrs. Parker put an arm around her. "You know Mrs. Scanlon would never send you off to visit people who aren't nice. I'm sure she's checked them out thoroughly."

"I'm not scared," Josie said, but her voice was hollow. "I can take care of myself." She went to the sink and turned on the water full blast. Then she stuck a head of lettuce under the stream. While she broke up the lettuce, her thoughts began to wander.

"Josie, are you washing that lettuce or trying to drown it?"

Startled, Josie looked down. The sink had filled with water, and the head of lettuce was bobbing in it.

"Oh! Sorry. I was just thinking . . ."

"About what? These Morgan people?"

Josie turned off the water. "Nah." She grinned. "I'm thinking about their horses."

Down in the basement laundry room, Cat opened the washing machine, pulled out the wet towels, and thrust them into the dryer. Gathering up more dirty towels, she put them in the washing machine and measured out detergent. Then she slammed down the lid.

She groaned as she eyed the huge stack of towels still waiting to be washed. And piled on the dryer were clean sheets, which had to be folded. *How could there be this much?* she wondered. Did everyone save their dirty laundry for the days when she was on duty?

A freckle-faced boy appeared at the door. "What do you want, Joey?" Cat asked. She was in no mood to be bothered by a ten-year-old.

"There's a phone call for you."

Cat's bad mood vanished. "Thanks," she yelled as she ran out the door.

The phone was in the reception area outside Mrs. Scanlon's office. Ellen, the new counselor, was working in there. "Do I have a call?" Cat asked.

Ellen nodded. "Line two."

Cat hit the button. "Hello?"

"Hi Cat, it's Jill."

"Hi!" Cat felt a pleasant tingle rush through her. Jill Newman was one of the most popular girls at school, and Cat had been cultivating her friendship all year.

"Listen, I'm having a few kids over tonight for a cookout. Can you come?"

"I'd love to," Cat began, and then she paused. She didn't want to tell Jill she'd have to get special permission. "Um, there's something else I'm supposed to do, but I think I can get out of it. Can I call you back?"

"Sure. Talk to you later."

Cat hung up and smiled. This was the first time Jill had ever invited her over, but she'd heard about her great parties. Some of the coolest kids from school would be there.

"You look happy. Good news?"

She had forgotten that Ellen was in the room. "That was a girl from school inviting me to a cookout tonight."

"How nice! I don't know all the rules and procedures yet. I suppose you have to get some sort of permission."

Cat thought rapidly. If she could get Ellen to think a counselor could give permission . . . "Well, yes. Is it okay if I go?"

Ellen hesitated. "Gosh, I don't know. Is this common? I mean, are you girls usually given permission to do this sort of thing?"

"Oh, sure. As long as it's at someone's home and an adult's there. And we have to leave a name and number."

"How would you get there?"

"Usually a counselor takes us. But I'm sure I could get a ride back. Is it all right? Can I go?"

Ellen looked confused. "Well, I'm not sure, but—" Relief flooded her face as Mrs. Scanlon walked in. "Cat wants to know if she can go to a cookout tonight at a friend's home."

"Tonight?" Mrs. Scanlon shook her head. "Catherine, you know the rules. You have to ask permission twenty-four hours in advance."

"Cat, you didn't tell me that." Ellen's tone was reproachful.

"But I was only invited just now! I didn't know about it twenty-four hours ago."

"I'm sorry, dear. But you should tell your friends about our rules, so they'll know to give you some advance notice."

Oh, sure, Cat thought angrily. Remind all the kids at school that she was different, that she was an orphan and didn't have a normal life like them.

"Now, don't pout. I have some news that just might cheer you up."

Cat wasn't optimistic that anything Mrs. Scanlon could tell her would make up for missing Jill Newman's party. But it wasn't a good idea to get the director angry, so she pretended to look interested.

"There's a couple, Annie and Ben Morgan, who are interested in adopting. I've told them about you, and they've invited you to visit them for a couple of days."

At least Cat didn't have to go on faking interest. "What are they like?"

"Very nice. Attractive people. They just moved to Vermont from New York. Would you like to go meet them?"

Cat tried to sound casual, but it wasn't easy. "All right."

A few minutes later, after calling Jill and claiming

she couldn't get out of her previous engagement, Cat was back in the laundry room slaving away. But her mood had definitely improved.

If these Morgan people were from New York, they were probably rich and sophisticated. Lots of New York people had places in Vermont—big, fancy, country homes. "Cat Morgan," she said experimentally. It had a nice ring to it.

She actually found herself humming as she folded the sheets. With any luck at all, this could be the last time she'd have to do it.

Four

Cat slid into her seat in the dining hall and placed her lunch tray on the table. She didn't have to look under the bread to know what the sandwich contained. Wednesdays were always bologna and cheese.

Across from her the new girl, Trixie, was slurping her vegetable soup. She didn't say anything to Cat, which was a relief, because Cat wasn't in the mood for conversation. She wanted a few minutes to think before Becka and Josie arrived at the table.

Mentally, she explored the contents of her closet. What should she bring to wear for her visit? She wanted to look good—but not too good. Then maybe they'd take her shopping for new clothes.

Clothes, shoes, jewelry—the possibilities were overwhelming! Not to mention everything else that would be different there. No picking up trays of crummy bologna sandwiches and bringing them back to a conveyor belt. She'd be served elegant meals—by a maid, maybe. And she wouldn't be sharing a bedroom with two nerdy roommates.

What would my bedroom look like? Cat wondered. She envisioned a lovely canopy bed, a vanity table with a mirror surrounded by little lights. Maybe she'd have her own private bathroom, too.

Would the Morgans have a swimming pool? Not that many people in Vermont did, but it wasn't impossible. Jill Newman's family had one.

How her life would change if she was adopted! She'd be like Jill Newman, a pampered only child, getting anything she wanted. Even though she'd never been to Jill's home, she'd heard about her fabulous room with its color TV, stereo, private phone line, and huge walk-in closet. A thrill shot through her as she contemplated all the possibilities of her new life.

"What are you smiling about? I'll bet it's not the soup." Josie plunked her tray down with a bang. Becka followed close behind.

"Nothing," Cat said. She considered telling them about her upcoming visit. It would be fun to see them both turn green with envy. On the other hand, she'd have to listen to Becka whine about wanting a family. And Josie might start watching Cat like a hawk, looking for some way she could get her into trouble.

No, Cat decided. It was better that she keep it all to herself until the adoption was definite. Then she'd

46

spring it on them, giving them just enough time to recover from their shock to say good-bye.

She chewed on her sandwich without even tasting it. Her thoughts were miles away. Canopy beds and vanity tables floated across her mind. Then it dawned on her that the table was a lot less noisy than usual. And Josie was looking at her with the oddest expression.

"What are *you* staring at?"

"You," Josie replied. "By now you should be saying something like, 'This food is disgusting.' "

"Well, it is," Cat said. "But I've got more important things on my mind today."

"Yeah? Like what? Wait, let me guess. You're trying to decide what color to paint your fingernails this week."

Cat wasn't about to dignify that with a response. But she peered under the table at her hand. What color *should* she use? Well, she couldn't decide that until she figured out what clothes she'd be wearing.

She noticed something else that was odd today. Becka wasn't wolfing her food down as usual. Instead, she was staring off into space and chewing on her nails. Cat was about to point out that this was a nasty habit but changed her mind. She was feeling too generous. After all, she was the one who was going off to a fine new home. They were stuck here. She could almost feel sorry for them.

She took a few sips of her soup, but she really wasn't hungry. She wanted to get up to the room alone so she could go through her closet without the others wondering what she was doing.

"Where are you going?" Josie asked as Cat rose.

Cat couldn't resist giving her a mysterious smile. "I've got something to do." After she left, Josie turned to Becka.

"Are you okay?"

Becka emerged from her fog. "Sure. Why?"

"You're so quiet. Don't get me wrong, it's nice for a change. But I thought you might be sick or something."

"No, I'm fine." Becka scolded herself for wearing her heart on her face. She couldn't tell Josie why she was being so quiet. In fact, she was afraid to talk at all, about anything. If she did, she might slip and end up telling Josie about her possible adoption.

Now Josie was *really* looking at her strangely. "You sure you're okay? You look weird."

Becka got up abruptly. She took a last longing look at her barely touched tray, but she didn't dare stay any longer. "I'm watching some of the little kids this afternoon. I better go pick out a book to read to them."

She knew Josie would be puzzled, especially by the fact that she hadn't finished her lunch. And she wondered how long she'd be able to keep this secret. Well, if she was going to be an actress, she'd better learn how to act. But she had had no idea it would be this difficult.

She didn't really have to watch the kids that afternoon. It had just been an excuse to get away. But she did head down to the TV room, where there was a bookcase filled with children's books.

It was a nice place to hide in the middle of the day, when there weren't groups of kids gathered around the TV. She liked poring through the books, particularly the ones counselors had read to her when she was younger. Like the one about the mouse who had to rescue his mother from the cat and spring his father out of a trap.

And the fairy tales. She could relate to Hansel and Gretel being sent away from home and trying to find their way back. *Rumplestiltskin* was another favorite story. She loved the part where the mother tried to guess the ugly creature's name so she could keep her baby.

She was sitting cross-legged on the worn carpet turning pages when Ellen walked in. She was lugging a huge box, which she placed on a table.

"What's that?" Becka asked.

"Clothes," Ellen told her. "And they're not even used. A department store in town donated them. I think they're mostly junior sizes, so Mrs. Scanlon said you and Cat and Josie should get first crack at it."

"Neat!" Becka exclaimed, jumping up.

"Cat's on her way. I think Josie's outside. I'll go find her."

Becka was itching to tear the box open immediately, but she thought she should wait for the others before grabbing anything for herself. Cat ran in just then and headed directly for the box.

"They're new clothes," Becka said excitedly. "Never even worn before."

"I know, Ellen told me." Cat started ripping the tape that encircled the box.

"Don't you think we should wait for Josie?"

"No." Cat tugged and pulled and finally got the box open. She tossed out some tissue paper and peered inside. "Ooh, this looks good!"

Becka watched as Cat started pulling items from the box. She wasn't quite as excited when she saw the contents. It looked like the kind of stuff Cat liked— plain and preppy, muted colors. But just as Cat pulled out a skirt, Becka saw something in the box that made her gasp in rapture.

It was a purple vest, trimmed in red, with gold and silver embroidery all over it. It was wild, colorful, and gypsyish—just the kind of thing Becka loved. "That's beautiful!" she cried.

Cat looked. "I want it," she said promptly, and snatched it out of the box.

"Cat! I saw it first!"

"*I* picked it up."

"But it would be so perfect with my long red skirt, the one I got at the flea market!"

"That rag?" Cat sniffed. "Shows how much you know about fashion. You don't wear a vest like this with some old-fashioned skirt. You wear it with a white shirt and jeans. It's a very hot look." She slipped it on. "And it fits me perfectly."

Becka was furious and on the verge of tears. "But you can wear all this other stuff. That's the only thing I like!"

Cat gave her one of her typical patronizing smiles. "Sorry, Becka, but I need it."

"For what?" Becka asked hotly. "Some party one of your stuck-up friends is giving?"

"No . . . okay, I'll tell you. Then maybe you'll understand." Cat came around the table to Becka's side. Then she did something extraordinary. She put her arm lightly around Becka's shoulders.

Becka looked at her in astonishment. When Cat spoke, her voice was unusually kind. "Now, I don't want you to feel bad about this. I know how much you want a family."

Becka eyed her suspiciously. "What are you talking about?"

"I've been invited to visit some people who want to adopt me. And I need this vest to dress up my jeans."

Any concern about the vest flew out of Becka's mind. "I'm going to visit a family, too!"

For a moment Cat just stared at her, speechless. Then she relaxed and her normal smug expression returned. "Oh Becka, you're just making that up because you're jealous."

"I am not! I *have* been invited to meet a family!"

"Sure you have." Cat removed her arm from

Becka's shoulders and went back to exploring the box.

Becka stamped her foot. "Okay, don't believe me! Just wait till you see me leave!"

Cat held up a blouse and examined it critically. "Only I probably won't be here to see that."

Becka gave up. Once Cat made her mind up about something, it was impossible to convince her otherwise. Besides, now she was worried about Josie. She was sure to find out that both Cat and Becka had been invited to visit families. Becka knew Josie would act like she didn't care. But how was she really going to feel, deep inside?

Josie sat on the floor of her room and rummaged through her bottom dresser drawer. It wasn't often that she got the room all to herself, and she wanted to take advantage of the privacy.

Finally she found what she was looking for—a plain brown envelope. She opened it and pulled out about a dozen snapshots.

They all featured the same people: A broad-shouldered, red-haired man wearing a cowboy hat. A slim, smiling woman in jeans, her brown hair carelessly pulled back in a ponytail. And a sturdy little girl with a mop of red curls and a crooked grin. Dad. Mom. Josie. In some of the photos there was a horse, a pretty golden-brown mare. Her name was Misty.

A familiar lump formed in Josie's throat as she studied the pictures. They all looked so happy, so safe and secure, totally unaware of the tragedy that awaited them.

Eight years had dimmed the memories, but fragments remained. Dad's jokes and his easygoing manner. Mom's quick laugh and her gentle touch. And little Josie, loved and cherished. A family.

Josie had long ago given up any hope of being part of a family again. But now she had this visit coming up. The thought of meeting two complete strangers who just might want to make her their daughter made her uncomfortable. No one could ever replace her mother and father.

And yet . . . Maybe the Morgans would be nice, in their own way. Maybe there would be something special about them. And if they were really special, maybe . . . just maybe . . .

Stop it, she ordered herself. *You don't know anything about these people. They could be awful. And if you go on this visit with great expectations, you'll just end up being disappointed.*

But even with this stern lecture, she couldn't still that tiny spark of optimism. To have it all again—a home, parents, not to mention horses.

There was a rap on the door. Hastily, Josie gathered up the photos and shoved them back in the envelope. "Come in."

The door opened and Ellen stuck her head in. "There's something down in the TV room you might find interesting."

"What?"

"Come on down and find out!"

Josie stuck the envelope back in the drawer and closed it. Then she followed Ellen downstairs. "Come on, give me a hint," she said.

Ellen smiled. "Don't you like surprises?"

"Not particularly." They went into the TV room, where Cat was trying on a jacket and Becka was holding a skirt to her waist.

"Oh. Clothes."

Ellen looked at her. "Aren't you interested in clothes?"

Cat eyed Josie's patched jeans and wrinkled T-shirt. "Isn't that obvious?"

"But wouldn't you like something nice to wear on your visit?" Ellen asked Josie. "Go on, take a look in the box." She left the room.

Josie was aware that both Cat and Becka were suddenly gazing at her strangely. "What visit?" Becka asked. "Where are you going?"

Josie shrugged nonchalantly. "To meet some family. Their name's Morgan." She was startled to see Becka go pale.

"Annie and Ben Morgan?"

"Yeah." She saw Cat's mouth fall open.

"That's who *I'm* going to visit."

"Me, too," Becka said.

They were all staring at each other now. Cat didn't bother to hide the annoyance in her voice when she spoke. "I thought it was just me going."

54

"Well, it's not," Josie said. "Looks like all three of us are invited."

The color was slowly returning to Becka's face, but she still looked stunned. "I wonder if we're all going separately or together."

Josie ambled over to the box and poked around inside. "Mrs. Scanlon said they're interested in adopting."

"Yeah, that's what she told me, too," Cat said.

"Me, too," Becka whispered.

Josie could actually feel the tension in the air. Very casually she picked a pair of socks out of the box and held them up. "I could use these."

No one put up an argument. In fact, no one said anything as they continued to look at the clothes. Josie felt pretty sure she knew why.

For years, they'd battled each other for one thing or another. They'd competed for attention, for clothes, for drawer space, use of the telephone, everything. Competition was nothing new for any of them.

But they'd never before had to compete for a family.

Five

"I can't get this thing shut!" Her face red with exertion, Cat glared at the suitcase as if it were deliberately refusing to close.

Josie, lying on her bed, peered over her magazine. "Why are you taking so much stuff?"

"Because I can't decide what to bring," Cat replied. "I want to be prepared for anything the Morgans have planned."

"Where do you think they're going to take you—to a ball?"

"You never know," Cat said, and smiled kindly at Josie. She could afford to be generous. After her initial dismay when she found out each of the roommates had been invited to visit, it had been a major relief to learn *her* visit would be first.

She pulled the suitcase onto the floor and sat on it,

trying to squeeze it shut. With all her might, she pressed on the locks to force them down.

Becka watched in alarm. "Cat, don't break it! We all have to use it."

Cat didn't respond. Becka didn't have to worry about that. If everything worked out the way she hoped, Becka wouldn't be going anywhere.

Finally Cat heard the locks click and she got up. Then she went to the mirror for a last-minute inspection. She'd gone easy on the makeup—the Morgans might be conservative. Now she turned this way and that, admiring how the light struck her hair. And the white sundress was perfect—casual but not *too* casual.

She knew the others were watching her, even though they were pretending not to. Josie couldn't resist a comment. "Good grief, Cat. This isn't a beauty contest."

Cat just smiled. This might not be a beauty contest, but it *was* a contest. And she was going to win. With effort, she lifted her suitcase. "Bye-bye," she sang out. At the door she added, "Don't miss me too much."

From the hallway she heard Josie call, "Don't worry about that!" She wasn't offended. After all, she wouldn't miss them either.

She lugged the suitcase down the stairs. When she reached the bottom, Mrs. Scanlon emerged from her office. "Good, you're all ready. Excited?"

Cat nodded.

"This will be the longest time you've been away

from Willoughby Hall," Mrs. Scanlon noted. "I hope you won't be homesick."

Homesick for Willoughby Hall? Cat very much doubted that. But she lowered her eyes demurely for Mrs. Scanlon's sake. "I'll try not to be."

"Have a wonderful time." Mrs. Scanlon bent down, and her lips brushed Cat's forehead. Cat was surprised. Mrs. Scanlon wasn't the kissing type. Maybe this was a good omen. Maybe Mrs. Scanlon thought she might not be seeing her again.

That fit in exactly with Cat's plans. She was going to do everything possible to charm the Morgans. She'd knock herself out to be the kind of daughter any parents would love to have. They would be so enraptured with her that they'd decide right then and there to adopt her. And they wouldn't even bother seeing Becka and Josie.

A couple of boys came bounding down the stairs. "Bill, Donnie," Mrs. Scanlon called to them. "Would you carry this out to the front steps, please?"

With a big show of grunts and groans, the boys hoisted the suitcase between them. Cat felt like a princess as she and Mrs. Scanlon followed them outside. *This is how it's going to be from now on,* Cat thought. *People doing things for me.*

"I'll wait with you so I can introduce you," Mrs. Scanlon said. Cat wasn't crazy about that idea—she wanted to be on her own. She didn't want Mrs. Scanlon's eyes on her as she went into her performance.

Fortune was smiling on her that day. Just then, a counselor came out. "Mrs. Scanlon, there's a phone call for you. It's long distance."

"Oh dear, I'd better take that. Cat, if they come while I'm gone, would you mind introducing yourself?"

"Not at all," Cat said graciously.

The two boys who had carried her suitcase were lingering around. As soon as Mrs. Scanlon went back inside, Cat turned to them. "Beat it," she hissed. The boys looked at each other, shrugged, and took off.

Cat lifted her hand and shielded her eyes from the sun, peering out at the road leading to Willoughby Hall. What kind of car would the Morgans have? Maybe a jazzy little sports car, or a convertible.

But what if they were *really* rich, richer even than Jill Newman at school? Closing her eyes, Cat visualized the car coming up the driveway. It would be a black—no, a white limousine. A uniformed man would step out. "Miss O'Grady? This way, please."

You're getting like Becka with her stupid fantasies, Cat told herself. But it was fun, so she kept her eyes closed and allowed her daydreams to continue.

After the ride, the car would turn into a circular driveway. From the window she'd see her new home rise up before her. A white mansion with columns . . . or maybe an ultramodern house, on different levels. Would there be a butler? Did people have butlers in real life, or was that just in the movies?

Her thoughts were interrupted by a chugging

sound. She opened her eyes. A battered blue station wagon was pulling into the driveway. She watched as a man with dark hair got out. From this distance, she couldn't make out his features, but he looked sort of young, like a friend of one of the counselors.

As he came walking up toward the door, she could see he wasn't quite so young. He was nice looking, though. He stopped at the steps and looked at her seriously.

"Are you Catherine O'Grady?"

"Yes."

"I'm Ben Morgan."

Cat looked at him blankly. *This can't be true,* she thought. Then, automatically, she stood up. "I'm pleased to meet you."

He smiled. "Is this your bag?" When she nodded, he lifted it. "Wow! What do you have, a rock collection?"

Cat uttered a tinkly laugh. She followed him to the station wagon and tried to sort out her thoughts. She'd read once in a magazine about a famous billionaire who drove around in an old jalopy to avoid publicity. Maybe Ben Morgan was like that.

"We've been looking forward to your visit," Ben said as he pulled out of the driveway.

"Oh, so have I! I've heard so much about you and Mrs. Morgan."

"Call us Ben and Annie. What have you heard?"

Cat racked her brain. What *did* she know about

them? "Well, I know you came from New York and you've just moved to Vermont."

Ben nodded, his eyes on the road. "Right, about three months ago."

"Do you like it here?"

"Very much. It's a lot more peaceful than New York."

Cat had never been to New York, but she'd seen the city on television. Privately she thought Vermont would be awfully boring after New York. "Why did you decide to move?"

"We wanted to make a real home. And we wanted to have our own business."

"What kind of business?"

"We have a store."

A store. That sounded promising. Cat pictured a gigantic department store, with MORGAN'S in neon lights.

Ben turned onto the expressway entrance ramp. "You'll have to excuse me if I can't carry on much of a conversation. I have to concentrate when I drive."

"That's all right," Cat assured him. She leaned back and closed her eyes. She hadn't had much sleep the night before. In her mind she saw herself skipping through a department store, grabbing anything that struck her fancy. . . .

She must have fallen asleep. It seemed like only seconds later when she dimly heard Ben say, "Well, here we are! Green Falls, Vermont."

Cat opened her eyes. *This must be Main Street,* she

thought. She noticed a bank, a pizza parlor, a beauty shop, lots of small boutiques. *No department store, though. It must be at the mall.*

"How far is the mall from here?"

"Mall?" Ben smiled. "We don't have one in this area. That's one reason Annie and I picked Green Falls. We wanted a real old-fashioned New England town." He turned off Main Street and onto a narrow, tree-lined road. "The house is just around the bend here."

Cat leaned forward and held her breath. Then, slowly, she exhaled. And as she let her breath out, she kissed her fantasies good-bye.

It wasn't a mansion. It wasn't even much of a house. What Ben was pulling up to was a gray, weather-beaten, two-story structure that needed a new coat of paint. Beat-up shutters framed the windows.

Even in her state of shock, she realized Ben was waiting for her to say something. "It looks . . . nice," she said lamely, getting out of the car.

Ben pulled out her suitcase, leaned against the car, and gazed at the place. "It's got potential. Needs a lot of work, though. That's why we want a family. More helping hands." Something must have shown in Cat's expression, because he laughed and quickly added, "Just kidding!"

But Cat was too dazed—no, *stunned*—to laugh. Wordlessly she followed Ben up some steps that creaked. As they reached the porch, the front door swung open. An attractive, young-looking woman with long, straight, brown hair stepped out. *Well,* Cat thought, *at least Annie isn't totally dowdy. She could be worse.*

"Welcome, Catherine! I'm Annie Morgan. Come on in."

Cat was afraid to see the inside of this dump. And her first sight of the living room confirmed those fears. The furniture was old and it didn't match. One wall was covered with chipped bookcases. The whole place looked dreary to her.

"I'll take your suitcase upstairs," Ben said.

"And I'll get lunch on the table. You must be starving!"

Cat wasn't. In fact, she'd totally lost her appetite. But she went with Annie through the dining room and into the kitchen anyway. "What do people call you?" Annie asked. "Cathy?"

"Cat."

"What a cute nickname. How did you get it?"

"I don't know."

Annie handed her a bowl. "Would you put this on the table, please?"

Just like Willoughby Hall, Cat thought. I even have to carry the food.

A few minutes later, the Morgans and Cat were sitting at the table. "I hope this tastes okay," Annie said, serving Cat what looked like a bean salad. "Ben and I are just learning to cook."

"Back in New York we lived on Chinese takeout," Ben explained.

Cat ate without even tasting it. She was trying to figure out how she was going to get through the next two days.

"What are you interested in?" Ben asked her.

Cat had expected a question like this, and she'd prepared an elaborate answer that would impress the Morgans. But now, what was the point? She shrugged. "I don't collect stamps or anything like that."

"Let me guess what interests you," Annie said. "Boys, clothes, music. How's that for a start?"

Cat's eyes widened, and Annie laughed. "I was thirteen myself once."

Cat sat up straighter. Maybe she should try to show *some* interest. She didn't want them telling Mrs. Scanlon she'd sat around sulking. "Um, what did you do back in New York?"

"I was in advertising," Ben told her. "And Annie was a fashion photographer."

Cat looked at her with new respect. "Really? That must have been so exciting!"

"Sometimes," Annie said. "But what I really wanted to do was paint. I have a studio out back. I'll show it to you."

"And bring her around to the store," Ben said. "Speaking of which, I'd better get back there. We just might get a customer." He got up. "I'll see you later, Cat."

64

Annie started clearing the table. Cat figured she was probably expected to help. And then they'd be washing dishes. What a drag.

But once the dishes were in the kitchen, Annie said, "I'll wash up. Cat, why don't you go change your clothes? That's a pretty dress, and you don't want to get it dirty."

Cat agreed, but she wondered what they'd be doing that could get her dress dirty. The possibilities weren't cheering.

"Come on, I'll show you your room."

By now Cat had given up any hope of a canopy bed and vanity table. *It's probably just a mattress on the floor,* she thought as she and Annie climbed the stairs.

But it wasn't as bad as that. It was a big room. The single bed had a pretty flowered spread, and there were matching curtains on the windows. The walls were a pale petal pink, and a darker pink rug was on the floor. The dresser and night table looked old, but they were painted a shiny white.

"We fixed this room up first," Annie said. "As soon as we started thinking about a family."

Well, it was an improvement compared to the rest of the house, Cat thought. But there was no TV, no stereo, no phone. What could she say about it? "It's . . . sweet."

"I'll leave you to change," Annie said, and closed the door behind her. *She's trying to be nice,* Cat thought grudgingly. *At least she believes in privacy.* Cat fell down on the bed, not caring if her dress got wrinkled. There didn't seem to be any reason to look nice here.

She'd never been so disappointed in her life. All her dreams and fantasies had been just that—dreams and fantasies. She got up and looked out the window, which faced the back yard. No tennis courts, no swimming pool . . . just a big old barn and a little shack, which was probably Annie's studio. She could see a vegetable garden, and beyond that she saw a horse.

That will give Josie a thrill, she thought. *And Becka will think everything here is just adorable.* Neither of them had any taste. Well, they'd get their precious visits now. Cat had absolutely no intention of allowing herself to be adopted. Let the Morgans have Josie or Becka. At least she'd be getting rid of *one* roommate.

But something bothered her. It was the idea of Josie or Becka thinking they'd won, that they'd beat Cat out for adoption. She couldn't stand that. True, there was no way *she'd* live here. But she wanted that to be *her* decision.

She jumped off her bed, opened her suitcase, and pulled out jeans, a shirt, and tennis shoes. As she dressed she decided she was going to be charming and sweet, just as she'd planned, and behave as if everything delighted her. She still wanted the Morgans to choose her. She just didn't plan to accept. And she'd make sure Josie or Becka—or whoever ended up here—would know she was second choice.

When Cat returned to the kitchen, Annie was placing the last dish in the drainer. "I like your jeans," she said. "They're Dandies, aren't they?"

Cat was surprised that Annie would know the name of the most popular brand, and it must have shown on her face. "I was in fashion, remember? I still try to keep up with what's going on."

Actually, now that Cat had a chance to look her over, she could believe that. Annie was wearing jeans —not Dandies, but obviously designer. Her man-tailored shirt was crisp and stylish. And the little scarf tied around her neck added a certain chic.

"Here, I'll give you the grand tour," Annie said.

"Great," Cat said, trying to sound more eager than she felt. *Grand* was hardly the word for what followed, but Cat gave the performance of her life. She admired Annie's studio, gushed over the mangy old horse, oohed and aahed over the tomatoes in the garden.

"Here's our barn." When Cat saw what was inside, she jumped back.

"They're just chickens," Annie said. "We have fresh eggs whenever we want them."

Cat eyed the birds askance, but she said, "They must be delicious."

Annie grinned. "Just between you and me, I can't tell the difference between these eggs and the ones you buy at the supermarket. Now I'll show you the store." As they went around to the front of the house, Cat started toward the car.

"Where are you going?"

Cat was confused. "I thought you said we were going to the store."

"We don't have to drive. It's right across the street."

Cat turned and looked. She hadn't even noticed it. And there was no reason she would have. The little building with MORGAN'S COUNTRY FOODS painted on the front was totally nondescript.

Inside, Ben was with a customer. Annie took Cat up and down the three aisles, pointing out the various items. "What do you think of our pride and joy?"

Cat didn't see much to take pride in. There were shelves lined with cans of maple syrup, jars of jellies and jams, and a table laden with baskets of fruits and vegetables that didn't exactly make her drool.

"Everything's completely natural," Annie explained. "There isn't one artificial ingredient or preservative, or even a teaspoon of sugar in this store."

"Wonderful," Cat murmured, but she wasn't really listening. She was looking at Ben's customer.

It was a boy, and he looked just a little older than she was. And he was *cute.*

"Annie, do we have any more apricot preserves?" Ben asked.

"They're in the storage room," Annie said. "I'll show you." They both went to the back of the store. The boy turned and saw Cat.

"Hi," she said, tossing her head so her hair would bounce around her shoulders.

68

"Hi," he replied. He looked at her with obvious interest. "You new around here?"

"Just visiting."

"Oh. Staying for a while?"

"No, just for a couple of days."

She was pleased that he seemed disappointed. Ben and Annie returned with some jars. "Here you go," Ben said, putting them in a bag and handing it to the boy.

"And tell your mother hello for me," Annie added.

"Thanks," the boy said. He went to the door and looked back at Cat. "Maybe I'll see you again."

Cat cocked her head. "Maybe."

Now why had she said that? She'd never be seeing that boy again. Too bad, though. He was really great looking.

She realized Annie was watching her, smiling. "He *is* cute, isn't he?"

Cat was taken aback. Was she a mind reader? Then she grinned. "Yeah. *Very.*"

"How do you like the store?" Ben asked.

"It's nice." Cat gazed around. "I guess you don't sell anything like makeup here, do you?"

"No, no makeup," Ben said.

Annie looked thoughtful. "You know, Ben, that's not such a bad idea. There are all kinds of natural makeups being made today. And shampoo, soap, bath salts—we might want to think about carrying stuff like that. Cat, I'll bet you could be a big help in picking

69

out those kinds of products. Are you interested in makeup?"

Cat nodded. "Sometimes I wear eyeshadow, but Mrs. Scanlon always tells me it's too much."

Annie studied her with interest. "Then you might like to see some stuff I've got back at the house. I used to help make up the models on my fashion shoots, and I've still got my case. You can do some wonderfully subtle things with the right shadows. Want to try it?"

Cat could think of worse ways to spend an afternoon. "Okay!" And with more enthusiasm than she'd felt since she'd arrived, she left the store with Annie.

Cat had expected the visit to drag on and feel like forever. But it didn't. It seemed like no time at all had passed when she found herself throwing her clothes back in the suitcase.

In all honesty, she had to admit it hadn't been as awful as she'd thought it would be when she arrived. Ben and Annie certainly seemed to like having her there. They couldn't do enough for her. Annie was really fun, too. And meeting that boy had been nice.

It was great having her own room for two nights, even if the room wasn't anything to get excited about. Looking around, she considered how she would redecorate it. Of course, that was silly. She'd never see it again.

Ben was at the door. "All set?"

"I just have to get this thing closed."

Ben came over and, with practically no effort at

all, closed the case and snapped the locks. Then he lifted it and carried it out.

Annie was waiting downstairs. "It's been wonderful having you, Cat."

"It's been wonderful being here. Thank you so much for everything you've done."

Outside, they all headed toward the car. Cat turned and took one last look at the house. Actually, it wasn't so awful. Once they fixed it up, it might even be presentable.

But she was glad the visit was over. Keeping up this charming act was getting exhausting. In a way it would be a relief to get back to Willoughby Hall, where she could just be herself again. Back where she wouldn't have to be so *nice*.

Six

Becka was trying very hard to keep absolutely still. Annie had already asked her twice not to move. But she was uncomfortable, sitting on the stool and posing as Annie drew her. She couldn't talk. She was afraid to even breathe too much. At least the enforced silence gave her the opportunity to sort out a jumble of thoughts.

She hadn't known what to expect when she arrived at the Morgans' yesterday. Cat hadn't given her or Josie any information about her visit. In fact, ever since she returned to Willoughby Hall two days ago, she hadn't said much of anything to either of them. She just went around with a smug, mysterious smile, like she knew something they didn't. Which, of course, she did. But thinking about Cat's behavior made Becka wonder if that smug smile meant some-

thing more. Maybe the Morgans had told Cat they
wanted to adopt her already. No, that couldn't be.
They would have canceled Becka's visit, and Josie's.

But if they *had* made their decision and decided
they wanted Cat, Becka wasn't so sure she'd mind.

"Becka, try not to change your expression, okay?"

Becka tried to murmur "Sorry" without moving
her lips. She wondered if she could move her eyes.
She let them stray slowly to Annie, then she brought
them back. Looking at Annie made her nervous.

Her thoughts went back to her arrival. Ben had
been nice on the trip, but awfully quiet. He'd told her
he couldn't talk because he had to concentrate on his
driving. And Becka was so afraid of being a chatter-
box that she'd barely said a word herself.

Driving through Green Falls had given her goose
bumps. It was just the kind of town she'd dreamed
about—quaint and charming and old-fashioned.

And the house fit into her fantasy, too. It was a
little run-down, but it had a comfortable, homey look.
When she saw the big porch, she pictured herself with
the Morgans, spending the afternoons sitting there,
drinking tea, greeting callers, having cozy little chats.

When Becka entered the living room, she imagined it in winter with a roaring fire. She would be
curled up in front of the hearth. Ben Morgan would
be reading aloud. Annie Morgan, dressed in gingham, would come in with a plate of homemade cookies and settle down to knit a scarf for her.

Then she met Annie Morgan. It didn't take long

for her to realize that this was not the kind of woman who would bake cookies all day, knit, or wear gingham dresses. Every time she looked at Annie, all Becka could think was that this was definitely not her idea of a mother. She looked so *modern*.

"Okay, you can breathe again!" Annie declared. "Come take a look."

Becka expected to see something soft and sweet, like those pictures she loved of girls with huge eyes. Instead she saw a sketch of someone who looked very ordinary.

"You don't like it," Annie said. "I can see it in your face."

Becka squirmed. This woman was so blunt! "No, I like it, I do," she insisted. She searched for a way to change the subject. "I've thought about becoming an artist."

"Really?" Annie lifted the sketch of Becka and exposed a clean sheet underneath. She handed Becka her piece of charcoal and said, "Draw something for me."

Becka stared at the charcoal in her hand and then at the blank sheet. She couldn't move.

"What's the matter?" Annie asked.

"I—I don't know how to draw."

She couldn't blame Annie for being puzzled. "But you said you'd thought about being an artist."

Becka fumbled with her words. "I just thought it sounded like a neat thing to be. I read a book about

74

an artist. It was very romantic. Anyway, I changed my mind. I want to be an actress now.''

"That's quite an ambition. Have you been in many plays at school?"

"Oh, no!" Becka exclaimed in horror. "To be in a school play you have to try out." She shuddered. "I couldn't get up and act in front of all those people.''

Now Annie looked really baffled. "But if you don't want to perform in front of people, why do you want to be an actress?"

Becka tried to explain. "I just thought it would be nice to play roles. You know, be someone else. . . .''

Annie smiled. "Sometimes it's nice just being yourself.''

Becka stared at the wood floor. Annie was making her uncomfortable.

"Come on, let's go outside," Annie said. As Becka stepped out the door, she almost tripped on her long skirt. Annie grabbed her arm to keep her from falling. "Are you sure you wouldn't like to change your clothes? You might be more comfortable in jeans.''

"I don't have any jeans. I don't really like them. No offense intended," she added quickly, eyeing Annie's jeans.

"None taken," Annie replied. "Becka, it's okay if you don't like everything here. You don't have to like my sketch, or my jeans, or even my cooking!" She laughed. "Even Ben's not too crazy about that!''

Becka managed a thin smile. She knew Annie was just trying to make her feel okay. But in the back of her mind she wondered, what was the point of being adopted if you didn't absolutely love everything about your new home?

Annie paused under the apple tree and picked two apples off the ground. "Let's go give Maybelline a treat."

Becka gulped. "Okay." They headed toward the horse who stood at the end of the field. Becka had only seen her from a distance. Up close, she was so *big*.

Annie tossed Becka an apple. "She'll eat it right out of your hand."

Becka hoped Annie couldn't see how squeamish she felt about this. Gingerly, Becka extended her arm, and the horse ambled over to her. Becka squeezed her eyes shut and steeled herself. But when she felt the rough tongue on her hand, she couldn't bear it. She dropped the apple and jumped back.

"Becka, Maybelline won't hurt you," Annie said gently.

Becka was too embarrassed to reply. At least Maybelline wasn't put off by her action. She lowered her head and ate the apple off the ground.

Annie tossed an arm lightly around Becka's shoulders. "I guess you're not used to being around large animals."

"Or even small ones," Becka admitted.

"That's too bad," Annie said. "Kids should have pets." Becka wasn't so sure about that.

Annie fed Maybelline the other apple. "Let's go over to the store and relieve Ben."

Becka gladly agreed. At least there wouldn't be any animals in the store.

But she was wrong. "Look what I've got," Ben announced when they walked in. He held up a tiny yellow kitten.

"Oh, Ben!" Annie exclaimed. "How adorable!" She took the kitten in her arms. "Where did you get her?"

"A kid came by selling them. And what's a country store without a resident cat?"

"Aren't you precious," Annie crooned to the kitten. "Becka, would you like to hold her?"

The animal looked pretty harmless. Becka thrust out her arms, and Annie placed the kitten in them. She felt soft and fluffy and purred contentedly.

"What shall we name her?" Annie asked. "Becka, do you have any ideas?"

Becka was pleased to be consulted. She looked at the kitten. Something about her reminded Becka of a sweet, innocent baby. "How about Aurora?"

"That's a beautiful name! Aurora it is. Ben, why don't you take a break? Becka and I will manage the store."

"Okay," Ben said. "See you later."

"I have to get some stuff out of the storage room," Annie told Becka. "Just yell if we get a customer."

A second after Annie disappeared into the back

room, the door opened and a woman walked in. "Hello. Do you have any blackberry jam?"

"I think so," Becka said. She put the kitten down and went to a shelf. Then she glanced toward the storage room. Should she call Annie? No, she decided, she'd handle this herself. Annie probably thought she was such a ninny, the way she'd been acting. This was a chance to prove herself. "Here it is."

"Oh, good." The woman picked up three jars and took them to the counter. She handed Becka some money. Becka opened the drawer where the money was kept and gave the woman her change. Then she put the jars in a bag and handed it to her.

The woman thanked her and left. Annie came out of the storage room. "Did I hear a customer?"

Becka nodded. "She bought three jars of jam. I took care of it."

"Good!" Becka basked in her approval. But just then the door opened and the woman came back in.

"I'm afraid this young lady gave me too much change." She handed two dollars and some coins to Annie.

"Thank you," Annie said. The woman gave Becka a reproving look and walked out.

Becka waited for the floor to open up so she could sink into it. When that didn't happen, she forced herself to look up. As she expected, Annie looked disturbed.

But she didn't say anything about the error. "Becka, your eyes are red."

"They are?" It dawned on Becka that her eyes felt itchy, too. And then she sneezed.

"Oh dear, I hope you're not coming down with something." She put a hand on Becka's forehead. "You don't feel feverish. But you'd better go back to the house."

"I don't feel sick," Becka protested.

"I don't want to take any chances," Annie said firmly. "Now go on."

Becka did as she was told. She really didn't mind. In fact, she liked the way Annie had spoken. It was sort of motherly. On the other hand, maybe Annie had just wanted to get rid of her before she made any more mistakes.

Back in the house, she saw Ben in the living room reading. He looked up and smiled. "Hi."

Becka stood there uncertainly. "Hi. Um, what are you reading?"

"It's *A Tale of Two Cities* by Charles Dickens. Have you ever read it?"

Becka shook her head. "Is it good?"

"One of my favorites. I guess this is the third or fourth time I've read it."

Becka drew her breath in sharply. "I do that, too! Read the same book over and over. Like *Jane Eyre*. I've read that at least three times."

"That's a great book. Is it your favorite?"

Becka thought about that. "It's one of them. But I

guess my all-time, number-one, favorite book is *Little Women.*"

"I've never read it," Ben said. "Tell me about it."

Becka's eyes widened. "Really?" She was always trying to tell Cat and Josie about the books she read!

When she finished, he said, "I can see why you like it so much."

"What's *A Tale of Two Cities* about?" Becka asked.

Ben told her. As he described the story, Becka could almost feel herself living two hundred years ago during the French Revolution. He was just getting to a really exciting part when Annie walked in with a big basket in her arms. Aurora was sitting on her shoulder.

"Help!" Annie called. Ben jumped up and grabbed the basket. "Mmm, peaches."

"A farmer came by selling them. I can make peach preserves."

"I've got an idea for something else, too," Ben said. "Remember that ice-cream maker our friends gave us when we left New York? Here's a chance to try it out. Why don't we make some peach ice cream?"

"Okay! And we'll have a cookout tonight. Becka, how does that sound to you?"

"Great," Becka said. Then Annie looked at her closely. "How are you feeling? Your eyes don't look red anymore."

"They don't itch, either. I guess I'm okay."

"That's good," Annie said. "Strange, though. I wonder what was wrong."

Becka wasn't sure, but she had a suspicion. She'd read about people who could just think themselves sick. Sometimes they didn't know what they were doing. It was subconscious, all in their heads, but the symptoms were real. Maybe that's what she had done to get herself out of the store.

She followed Annie to the kitchen, where she was put to work washing peaches. Ben let Aurora out the back door and followed her to go start the grill. Annie beat some eggs and gathered the rest of the ingredients.

Then they all gathered on the back porch where Ben had set up the ice-cream maker. While Annie and Becka sliced up the peaches, the kitten frolicked on the ground around their feet. *Aurora's cute now,* Becka thought, *but she'll grow into a cat with claws.* The thought wasn't very appealing.

"Who wants to crank first?" Annie asked as she piled the ingredients into the ice-cream maker.

"I'll do it," Becka volunteered.

Annie put a checked plastic cloth on the picnic table, Ben went back to the grill, and Becka started cranking. As she looked around, she realized that something about this scene looked familiar. Then she knew why. It was the kind of scene she'd fantasized about—a real family cookout. The smell of chicken on the grill, Annie's laughter as the kitten tried to jump on the table, Ben's silly apron that read KISS THE

COOK—it was like something out of a book. Only this time it was real life.

And then she screamed.

"Becka! What's wrong?" Annie and Ben ran over to her. Becka couldn't speak. She just pointed.

"Oh, it's just a frog!" Annie exclaimed. "Nothing to be afraid of," she said with a chuckle.

"There are lots of creepy crawlies around here," Ben said cheerfully. "You better get used to them."

"I was just startled," Becka said. "I'm not really scared of frogs." But she knew she didn't sound very convincing. She didn't like anything that creeped or crawled or jumped. And Ben was wrong. She didn't have to get used to them—unless they adopted her. And unless she wanted to be adopted by them.

Tomorrow she'd be going back to Willoughby Hall. Becka thought she'd be depressed thinking about it, but she wasn't. At least there she always knew what to expect. There were rules and schedules and routines. You even knew what kind of food you'd get for lunch each day.

There was something very comforting about that.

Seven

"Josie, these are *de*-licious!" Ben took another bite of his blueberry muffin and rolled his eyes in appreciation.

"I can't resist. I'm going to have another one," Annie said. "Mmm, I don't think I've ever had muffins this good. I wish I could make them like this."

"It's easy," Josie said, picking a blueberry out of hers and popping it in her mouth.

"Easy for you," Annie said mournfully. "It wouldn't be so easy for me. I just don't have the knack."

No kidding, Josie thought, remembering the dinner they'd had the night before. But she wanted to be kind. "It doesn't take talent. Just practice. The first time I made muffins, they were like rocks."

Ben wolfed down the rest of his and eyed the remaining ones with longing. "I wonder if we should start carrying muffins in the store."

Annie nodded. "If we could have some like these, I know they'd sell."

"I'll give you the recipe," Josie said. She was pretty sure she wouldn't be there to make them herself.

As they started clearing away the breakfast dishes, Annie asked, "How did you get to be such a good cook?"

"From watching Mrs. Parker at Willoughby Hall. I help her in the kitchen. It's one of my regular duties."

Annie paused in the midst of scraping off what little remained on one of the plates. "You girls have to do a lot of chores there, don't you?"

"Yeah, I guess so." Then Josie was afraid she was giving the wrong impression. "Well, not that much. It's not like we're slaves or anything."

Annie was still clutching the half-scraped plate and looking at her. "You went to Willoughby Hall when you were about six years old, right?"

"Yes."

Ben put a hand on her shoulder and Josie winced. "Then you remember what it was like to have a home."

"Yes." She took a deep breath. "Willoughby Hall's okay. I mean, there are a lot of worse places an orphan can be." She immediately regretted saying that. She didn't want them asking how she knew.

She went to the sink and turned on the water, but Annie stopped her. "Hey, this is your holiday. No chores for you, young lady. Why don't you go outside? We'll be out in just a few minutes."

"Okay." Josie went out onto the back porch. She was glad to escape them, even if just for a few minutes. She didn't want to talk about her past, and she didn't want to talk about Willoughby Hall. She particularly didn't want to talk about Mrs. Parker. Even though Josie had only been away for twenty-four hours, she missed Mrs. Parker terribly.

You're such an ingrate, she scolded herself. The Morgans had been awfully nice to her, and here all she wanted to do was get away from them. Maybe it was because it had been a long time since she'd had so much attention. She wasn't sure she liked it.

Of course, the Morgans might not be as nice as they seem, she thought. It could all be a big act. She'd known people who could be sweet as honey on the surface, then turn around and stab you in the back. She had to admit that Annie and Ben didn't *seem* like phonies. But you never knew.

She paced the length of the porch restlessly. Then she leaned against the railing and gazed out at the field. Becka had said the Morgans lived in "the country." Josie had been dumb enough to believe her.

Josie had envisioned miles and miles of land in the middle of nowhere. But this? This was within walking distance of Main Street. Sure, there was some land, a barn, a garden, and an old nag who was a poor excuse

85

for a horse. But this wasn't what Josie would call country. It was just an ordinary house in an ordinary small town. At least the house was pretty comfortable. But Josie wasn't taken in by the homey touches. She knew that the Navajo rugs and the old-fashioned weather vane probably came from Macy's.

It had been a major disappointment when she arrived yesterday. But it was her own fault for having fantasies. She should have known better than to expect everything to be the way she wanted it to be. Or to expect Annie and Ben to be who she wanted them to be.

Just then, Annie and Ben joined her on the porch. "What a gorgeous day," Annie remarked.

It wasn't a question, but Josie knew she was supposed to say something in return. "Yeah, real nice."

"I'm still thinking about those muffins," Ben said in a dreamy voice. "Josie, have you ever considered becoming a professional chef when you grow up?"

"Nah. Cooking's fun, for a hobby. But I want to work outdoors."

"Doing what?" Ben asked.

Josie didn't really want to talk about her personal dreams in front of two almost strangers. But she couldn't be rude. "Something with horses. Like a groom or a jockey. What I'd really like to do . . ." She stopped.

"What?" Annie asked. "Tell us."

Josie knew they wouldn't approve, but they might as well know what she was really like. "What I'd really like to do is quit school as soon as I can and join a rodeo."

As she expected, Ben looked horrified. "Drop out of school?"

"Not till I'm sixteen," Josie added quickly. "That's the earliest you can do it."

"But don't you want an education?" Annie asked.

"Not particularly. I'm not into books and stuff. I'd rather just be with horses."

"Have you ridden much?" Ben asked.

Josie shook her head in regret. "Not since I was a little kid in Texas. Except for two years ago at a county fair. But that doesn't count."

"Would you like to ride Maybelline?" Annie asked. Before Josie could respond, Ben spoke up.

"I don't know, Annie. If she hasn't been on a horse in a while, it could be dangerous."

Josie stifled a smile. From what she'd seen of Maybelline, riding her would be about as dangerous as riding a carousel horse. "I think I could manage it."

Ben still looked doubtful, but he nodded. "I'll get the saddle," he said, and went out toward the barn. Josie and Annie headed across the field to where Maybelline was grazing. Josie stroked her mane.

"Want to go for a ride?"

In her opinion, the horse looked totally uninterested. Ben joined them then with the saddle. "Want me to put this on for you?"

"I can do it," Josie said.

"Do you know how?" Annie asked. "Surely you couldn't have been saddling your own horses when you were in Texas."

"No," Josie admitted, "but I know how to do it. I've got this book I memorized." Ben caught her eye and grinned.

"You mean you actually read books sometimes?"

Josie blushed. "Yeah, well . . . I guess some books are okay."

Ben watched as she saddled Maybelline. Then he made sure everything was adjusted properly. "Good job."

Josie thrust her foot in a stirrup and hoisted herself up. "Just ride as long as you want," Annie called up to her.

"Giddyap," Josie said, holding the reins firmly. Maybelline amiably began walking. Even though this wasn't much of an animal, Josie still felt exhilarated just being on a horse again. She jiggled the reins a bit, trying to work Maybelline up to a trot. But a lazy walk was about all the horse was up for, and Josie had to be content with that.

Looking out over the field, she knew that it wasn't her idea of a spread. And Annie and Ben weren't really farm people. Even in jeans they both still looked citified. And Annie especially looked forbiddingly put together. Not Josie's kind of people. But they did seem to like her. Unless it was just an act, she reminded herself.

But could she be happy here? she wondered. She

quickly wiped that question from her head. No, this wasn't what she wanted. Besides, Ben probably preferred Becka, who read all the time. And she was sure Annie liked Cat better than her.

Since they were in a fenced-in field, Josie didn't bother to steer Maybelline—she just let her roam in any direction she wanted. Now Maybelline was heading toward a figure sitting on the fence, way over on the other side of the field.

As they got closer, Josie realized what the attraction was. The boy on the fence was holding something out in his hand. Trying not to stare, Josie gave him a once-over.

He was tall and lanky, and he looked about her age. His hair was red—not dark red like hers, but a bright, fiery orange-red. And he had tons of freckles.

"Hi," he said as Maybelline edged toward him.

"Hi," Josie replied. She looked down at the boy's hand. There were several sugar cubes in it.

"Maybelline loves these," he explained. That was obvious, as the horse nuzzled his hand and wolfed down the cubes.

"Are you visiting Annie and Ben?" he asked.

"Yes. I'm Josie Taylor."

"I'm Red MacPherson." He stuck his hand in his jeans pocket and pulled out more sugar cubes. "I live on the next farm. You a relative of the Morgans?"

"No." She decided she might as well explain. After all, she'd probably never see him again. "I live at Willoughby Hall. It's an orphanage."

"You're an orphan?"

She was pleased to see that he didn't automatically look sympathetic. He was just curious.

She grinned. "Well, I wouldn't be living in an orphanage if I wasn't."

Red's face went a little pink. "Yeah, I guess that was a dumb question. Are the Morgans going to adopt you or something?"

"I doubt it," Josie said. "They invited two other girls out, too. Becka and Cat. They've already been here."

"You mean they're going to choose one of you to adopt?"

"Or none of us. I don't know."

Red's pocket seemed to hold an endless supply of sugar cubes. He pulled out another one. "That must feel kind of weird. Like you're here on approval or something."

Josie shrugged. "It doesn't bother me. They'll probably pick one of the others anyway."

He cocked his head and eyed her quizzically. "Why do you say that?"

Josie couldn't believe she was being so open and forthright with this total stranger. Maybe it was the red hair. "Well, Cat's real pretty and charming. Adults like her a lot. And Becka's smart. She reads all the time."

"That's enough sugar for you," Red said as he fed Maybelline the last cube. He searched the ground. Then he hopped off the fence and picked up an apple.

He held it out to Maybelline, who gnawed at it. "What about you?"

"Huh?"

"You say Cat's pretty and Becka's smart. What are you?"

Josie shrugged. "I don't know. I guess I'm pretty ordinary. Just a regular kid."

"Maybe that's what Ben and Annie are looking for. A regular kid. This is a pretty ordinary kind of place." He grinned. "I'll bet you'd fit in around here."

Josie shifted in her seat. "Yeah, well . . . Nice talking to you." Maneuvering the reins, she turned the horse around and started back toward the house.

That was a weird conversation, she thought. That guy didn't even know her. How could he say she'd fit in here? How did anyone ever know where they'd fit in?

After dinner that evening they all sat around in the living room. Annie was on the floor, stripping the finish off an old rocking chair she'd found at a flea market. Ben brought out a guitar and began singing some old folk songs.

"I wish it was winter, and we could have a fire," Annie said. But with the windows open and the fresh, clean, Vermont air pouring in, Josie thought everything was fine just the way it was.

". . . I'm five hundred miles away from home," Ben sang. He didn't have a great singing voice. In fact, he was kind of flat. But still, that song stirred something in Josie. Sitting on the floor, her arms wrapped around her knees, she hummed along. A small yellow kitten sat in front of her and seemed to be purring in time with the music. Josie had rolled her eyes when she'd heard the cat's name. "Aurora" had to be Becka's influence.

". . . Away from home, away from home . . ." Ben sang.

Home, Josie thought. *This feels like a home. Could it feel like* my *home?*

She gritted her teeth. *Stop that,* she ordered herself. *Don't start thinking that way. Don't get your heart set on something you can't count on.* Besides, she wasn't even sure she wanted this to be her home. She didn't know if she could be happy here. And nobody was going to give her any guarantees.

She still didn't believe Annie and Ben were the kind of people they seemed to be. There was only one person Josie completely trusted in the world—Mrs. Parker. And she was back at Willoughby Hall.

Annie got up from the floor and stretched. "I think that's enough work for tonight." She flopped down on the sofa. "I'm beat."

"I'm pretty sleepy myself," Ben said. He set the guitar down. "I'm going to turn in early." He kissed Annie and came toward Josie. Josie stiffened as he kissed her forehead. "Good night, Josie."

"Good night," she murmured. He went upstairs.

"You know what?" Annie said in a sleepy voice.

"I'm absolutely craving one of those brownies you made us for dessert."

"I'll go get you one," Josie said. She got up and went to the kitchen. But when she returned with the brownie, Annie's eyes were closed.

Josie watched her for a minute. Then, on tiptoes, she made her way over to Ben's guitar. She picked it up and carried it out the door to the front porch.

Her mother had played the guitar. Josie had a dim memory of falling asleep in her father's arms while her mother sat on the porch, strumming and singing in her sweet voice. A couple of years ago at Willoughby Hall there had been a counselor who played the guitar. He'd taught Josie a few basic chords and some simple songs.

She remembered where to place her fingers on the strings, then did one tentative strum. Then she looked behind her through the screen door. Annie was still lying there asleep.

Josie began to play, and she sang softly, "Michael, row the boat ashore, alleluia." She looked up at the sky. The stars twinkled down on her as she continued her song.

It was so beautiful, so peaceful. The noisy corridors of Willoughby Hall, the constant squabbles with Cat and Becka—it all seemed far away.

"You have a lovely voice, Josie."

Josie's fingers froze and she stopped singing. She turned to see Annie standing at the door.

"Don't stop," Annie said. "Keep singing."

Josie got up. "I'm tired. I think I'll go to bed." She went past Annie and started up the stairs.

Boy, I must have sounded rude, she thought. Well, it didn't matter. She'd be leaving tomorrow. She'd thank them politely, give Annie the recipes she wanted, and say good-bye. And that would be the end of that.

Eight

Josie waved to the blue station wagon as it pulled away. For a moment she stood there, watching it disappear around a bend in the road. Then, tossing her knapsack over her shoulder, she walked up the steps and into Willoughby Hall.

The entrance hall had never looked so good to her before. She gazed with new appreciation at the threadbare rug, the chipped table by the door, the mirror on the wall. From the television room, she heard the squeals of the little kids watching *Sesame Street*. A second later, a bunch of noisy little boys, sweaty from playing outdoors, came tearing by and practically knocked her down.

She didn't care. It was all wonderfully familiar.

Ellen came out of Mrs. Scanlon's office. "Hi! Did you have a good time?"

"Yeah, fine. Will you sign me back in?" She ran upstairs to her room. Even *that* looked good to her, especially since no one else was there. She dropped her pack on her bed, went back downstairs, and headed directly to the kitchen. She'd planned on running in and throwing her arms around Mrs. Parker. Instead, she stood in the doorway and frowned.

Mrs. Parker's back was to her. "Cat, stir this for a while."

"What's *she* doing in here?" Josie asked.

Cat looked up. "Doing *your* job."

Mrs. Parker wiped her hands on her apron and came over to give Josie a hug. "I missed you, child! How was your visit?"

Josie was conscious of Cat's eyes on her. "Good. Better than good, even. Cat, give me that bowl. You're not stirring it right."

"Tell us what you did," Mrs. Parker commanded.

"Well, I made them blueberry muffins. And brownies. The kind with the walnuts. They loved 'em. Ben thinks I should become a professional chef. I told them I learned everything from you."

Mrs. Parker smiled. "Flattery will get you everywhere. Cat, what are you doing?"

Josie looked. Cat had her face practically pressed against the silver-colored toaster. "I'm trying to see how my eyes look."

"Like they always look," Josie said.

"No, they don't," Cat replied. "They look different. Annie showed me how to use eye shadow to

96

make them bigger. She knows a lot about makeup. And she gave me a bunch of stuff to take back here.''

"Is that how you spent your visit?" Josie asked scornfully. "Putting on makeup?"

"I'll bet it was more fun than slaving in the kitchen," Cat retorted. "Becka, what do *you* want?"

Becka was standing in the doorway, her face buried in a book. She didn't appear to have heard Cat.

"Becka!" Mrs. Parker said loudly. Becka looked up.

"Oh! Hi."

"Are you here for a reason, or just visiting?" Mrs. Parker asked.

"I'm supposed to tell you something," Becka said. "Um, um . . . oh yeah, Mrs. Scanlon wants to see you about planning meals for next week."

Mrs. Parker took off her apron and started out of the kitchen. But she turned back and gave the three girls a keen look. "No wars in my kitchen, girls."

"What did she mean by that?" Becka asked.

Josie understood. Mrs. Parker was so wise. She could always sense when there was tension in the air.

Becka sat down at the kitchen table. "What did you do at the Morgans?"

"She cooked," Cat snorted.

"That's not all I did," Josie objected. "I rode their horse, Maybelline."

Becka wrinkled her nose. "I tried to feed her an apple. But she was so big, I got nervous and dropped it."

"They must have thought you were a real wimp," Cat said. "What did *you* do there, sit around reading the whole time?"

"No," Becka said. "But Ben and I talked about books. He loaned me this one. It's *David Copperfield.*"

"I'm so impressed," Cat said, dripping sarcasm.

"And Annie drew a portrait of me," Becka added.

Josie couldn't help grinning when Cat looked up sharply. "She did?"

Becka nodded. And with a smile so smug it could *almost* rival Cat's, she got up and sauntered out.

Later, as she read aloud to some kids in the TV room, Becka recalled Cat's expression. It had been fun seeing *her* look envious for a change. It didn't mean anything, though. There was no way of knowing who the Morgans had liked best. It *could* be her, she thought. But if it wasn't, how much would she care?

"Becka!" cried a plaintive voice. "Don't stop reading!"

"Sorry," Becka said. She tried to concentrate on the story and read the page with expression. Then she held the open book out to the kids so they could see the picture.

She smiled as they oohed over it. She loved doing this. If she left, she'd miss reading aloud. She'd miss the kids, too. They made her feel important.

She finished the book just as a counselor came in. "Okay, guys, time to wash up for dinner."

As the younger children scampered out, Becka asked, "What's for dinner tonight?"

"Fried chicken," the counselor told her.

Becka was pleased. Mrs. Parker made great fried chicken. In fact, a person could always count on good food at Willoughby Hall. She remembered the meals she'd had at the Morgans and wrinkled her nose.

When Becka got to the dining hall she went to her regular seat. Cat and Josie were already there. Becka put her tray on the table, sat down, and positioned *David Copperfield* in front of her. Peering over the top, she could see Trixie looking at her. Then Trixie's eyes darted to Josie and Cat.

"What do *you* want?" Cat asked.

"You all went on your visits, right?"

"Yeah, so what?" Josie asked.

"I'm trying to figure out who got picked."

"None of your business," Cat snapped.

Becka explained. "They haven't decided yet, Trixie."

"They probably won't want any of you." Trixie snickered.

Donna, a girl sitting next to Trixie, looked puzzled. "What are you talking about?"

"Some family had all three of them out for visits. But I don't think any of them are going to get adopted." Trixie pointed to Cat, Josie, and Becka. "She's a snob, she's a slob, and she's just plain goofy."

Poor kid's jealous, Becka thought. She spoke kindly.

"Trixie, we've been here a lot longer than you have. You'll have a chance to be adopted someday."

"I *told* you, I *can't* be adopted. I've got parents."

"Yeah, right," Cat muttered.

"I'll tell you something else, too," Trixie added. "Having parents isn't all that great sometimes."

"What do you mean?" Becka asked.

Trixie suddenly became very interested in her food. "Never mind."

Donna jumped into the conversation. "I know what she means. I was almost adopted last year."

"Yeah, I remember that," Josie said. "Didn't you stay with some family for a month?"

"Yeah. It was awful. They watched me constantly, wouldn't let me out of their sight. It was like being in prison. They drove me crazy."

"What did you do?" Becka asked.

Donna spoke with pride. "I threw a fit and it freaked them out. They couldn't deal with me, so they sent me back."

Becka gazed at her for a minute. Then she went back to her chicken. "Ben and Annie wouldn't be like that," she said between mouthfuls.

"How do you know?" Josie asked suddenly. "We don't know them at all."

"You better know them really well before you let them adopt you," Donna said wisely.

Some other kids at the table were listening to the conversation. "Who's getting adopted?" a boy asked.

"Some family's thinking of adopting one of them," Donna said.

The boy made a face. "I wouldn't want to be adopted. Remember Marty Stewart? He was adopted two years ago. I saw him at the park this summer."

"How's he doing?" Donna asked.

"Not too good. He said all his new parents want is a workhorse. They've got him cleaning the house, working at his father's garage, and baby-sitting their baby. He thinks the only reason they adopted him was to get a free servant."

"That's gross," Josie said.

Cat looked at her thoughtfully. "Didn't you say the Morgans made you cook all day?"

"They didn't *make* me."

"I had to work in their store," Becka said. "Well, I guess I didn't *have* to. I could have said no. But I think they expected me to do it."

Cat was rapping her nails on the table. "Ben made this joke about needing more helpers, and that's why they wanted a family. At least, I thought it was a joke."

Suzy, a ten-year-old, piped up. "Parents can be horrible. This girl I know at school gets punished if she gets anything less than an A on her report card. Sometimes she's grounded for *months.*"

"I heard something worse than that," a boy at the end of the table said. "There's a boy in my class whose parents locked him in the basement for a week."

"That's child abuse!" Becka exclaimed.

"I don't believe you," Josie told the boy.

"It's true," he insisted. "At least, that's what he said. It's really weird. I saw his parents once at school, and they looked so normal."

"That's how it can be," Trixie said. "Parents can look normal on the outside and be monsters inside."

Donna agreed. "Personally, I'd just as soon stay here. At least in a place like this, there are rules about how kids can be treated. They can't hit us or make us work too hard. Once you have parents, they own you. They can make you do anything."

"Or do anything *to* you," Suzy added darkly.

Becka could feel her heart thumping rapidly. She tried to read her book, but she couldn't concentrate on the words. She looked at Josie. Josie was staring into space, not even eating. Then she looked at Cat and almost gasped.

Cat was biting her nails.

The next morning Cat was dusting the frame around the mirror in the entrance hall. Her thoughts kept going back to the stories she'd heard at the dinner table the night before. They had to be lying, she thought. But why couldn't she get the stories out of her mind?

She looked at herself in the mirror. The vision seemed to blur, and suddenly she saw herself, thin and haggard, on her hands and knees scrubbing a floor. A regular Cinderella.

102

She blinked and the vision cleared. *You're being silly,* she told herself. *You've never had to scrub a floor.* At Willoughby Hall, there was a cleaning person who did the big jobs. But who knew what the Morgans would expect of her? And what if they were really strict and wouldn't let her date or go to dances or have any fun at all?

A counselor came in the front door with the mail. "Cat, here's something for you." She handed her a postcard.

Cat looked at the picture first. It was a beach scene. Then she turned it over. It was from Felicia, a girl in her homeroom. She was on vacation with her parents in Florida. The Morgans probably never went to places like Florida, Cat thought.

The message on the card was brief. "Having a great time. Lots of cute boys. I'm planning a big picnic for Labor Day, so put it on your calendar!"

Cat smiled with satisfaction. Felicia was neat, one of the popular kids. It hadn't been easy for Cat to break into that crowd. Being an orphan didn't help. But Cat had done it. She'd played up to the best people and worked her way into acceptance. Now she was finally where she wanted to be. If she was adopted, she'd have to start all over again at a new school.

She picked up her dusting spray and cloth and went into the television room. "Becka, what are you doing?"

"Dusting."

103

"But I've got dusting today!"

Becka turned. "You do?"

Cat put her hands on her hips. "Didn't you look at the duty schedule?"

"I thought I did," Becka said vaguely.

Josie came into the room and sat down at the table. She placed a sheet of paper on it and started chewing on the pen she was holding. "I hate writing letters," she muttered.

"Who are you writing to?" Becka asked.

"I have to do my thank-you note to Annie and Ben." She stared at the paper. Then she quickly scrawled something.

Cat looked over her shoulder. "Is that all you're writing?"

"It's enough," Josie said. She read aloud. " 'Thank you for having me visit. I had a very nice time.' "

"Brilliant," Cat said.

"Shut up," Josie replied.

Just then Trixie ran in. "Hey, I just remembered something else I heard about a kid who was adopted. There was this girl who was adopted by a family. And they seemed really nice. Only after she went to live with them, she found out they were part of a devil cult. And they were planning to use her for a human sacrifice!"

"That was a *movie*," Cat said. "I saw it, too."

Trixie grinned and ran back out.

"What a dork," Cat said. But Josie wasn't listening. She was staring at Becka.

"Becka! Are you crying?"

Sure enough, Cat could see the tears streaming down her face. "Good grief, you don't *believe* that crazy story, do you?"

Becka sniffled and rubbed her eyes. "I guess not. It's just that . . ."

"What?" Josie demanded.

"If . . . if the Morgans choose me, I don't know if I want to be adopted. I think I want to stay *here.*"

"Well, I wouldn't worry about it if I were you," Cat said. "I doubt that they'd choose you over me."

"Will *you* go if they choose you?" Josie asked.

"I don't know." But she did—and she might as well tell them now. "No. I don't want to live on that dinky farm and work in that dumb store." She paused. "I guess that leaves you, Josie."

Josie chewed on her pen. "I don't think I want to be adopted either. I'm not saying I believe all those stories about rotten parents. But still, you don't know what you're getting into if you let yourself get adopted. At least here I know what's going to happen."

Becka wiped away her last tear. "Yeah, that's what I think, too."

The room fell silent as the girls eyed each other uneasily. "What are we going to do?" Becka finally asked. "I mean, if they ask one of us, what's our excuse?"

"We'll need three excuses," Josie said. "Because if

the first person they ask says no, they'll probably ask another one of us. And so on.''

Cat considered that. She couldn't see herself telling them they weren't rich enough for her. There had to be something else she could say that would explain why she didn't want to be adopted.

"I've got it!'' she said suddenly. "And we won't even need three excuses. Just one.''

"What?'' Becka and Josie asked in unison.

Cat was amazed by her own brilliance. "We'll tell them we don't want to be separated! We'll say we're a team, and we have to stay together.''

The stunned expressions on her roommates' faces didn't surprise her. "That's crazy,'' Becka said. "No one would believe that!''

"Look, they don't really know us,'' Cat argued. "As far as they're concerned, we could be best friends. Like sisters, even.'' She began pacing the floor. "When they say, 'Cat, we'd like to adopt you,' I'll just say, 'Gee, thanks, but I have to stay with Josie and Becka. We're a team.' ''

Josie made a gagging sound. Cat turned to her with flashing eyes. "You got a better idea?''

Becka sat down. "You know, it just might work. We'll tell them we're like the Three Musketeers.''

"Who are they?'' Cat asked.

"They're in a book. Ben would understand. Okay, let's do it. If they ask me, I'll say I can't leave you guys.''

Josie still looked doubtful. "I don't know how I'm going to say that with a straight face."

"You probably won't need to," Cat replied. "Unless they want a cook more than a daughter."

Josie started to stick out her tongue, but pulled it back in as the door opened.

"Hello, girls," Mrs. Scanlon said. "I'm glad you're all here. The Morgans just called. They'd like to take all three of you on a picnic Sunday."

Becka raised her eyebrows. "All three of us?"

"Yes. Obviously you all made a good impression on them. I'm proud of you." She walked out.

Josie frowned. "Now what? Do we give them our excuse at the picnic?"

Cat thought about that. "No . . . we better save that as a last resort." She sat down and considered the possibilities. "Wait a minute. There's something else we can try at the picnic. Something that might keep them from even inviting any of us."

"What?" Becka asked.

Cat leaned back on the sofa and smiled. "It's simple. We can just be three people *nobody* would want to adopt."

Nine

Becka had her doubts about Cat's scheme. It was so outrageous. "Do you think we can pull it off?" she asked Josie Sunday morning in their room.

"Sure," Josie said, but she didn't sound all that confident.

"But don't you think it's kind of, I don't know . . . mean? The Morgans were awfully nice to us, and—"

"You want them to adopt you?" Josie interrupted. "No."

"Then we better go along with Cat's idea." She got up. "I have to go make those brownies."

Becka wrinkled her nose. "You're really going to do what you said you'd do?"

"Fits in with the plan, doesn't it?"

Becka sighed. "Yeah. I guess so."

Josie left, and Becka thought about the upcoming picnic. If Cat's scheme worked, there was no way Annie and Ben Morgan would want any of them. But Becka worried about playing her part.

Well, she'd *said* she was going to be an actress someday. Here was her chance to prove she could be.

Cat came into the room with a brown paper bag. "I'm going to start getting ready," she announced. She stood in front of the mirror. "This isn't going to be easy. And I hope I don't run into anyone I know."

Becka watched in fascination as Cat went to work. First, she pulled a bottle out of the bag.

"What's that?" Becka asked.

"Vegetable oil. I swiped it from the kitchen." She poured a little into her cupped hand. Then she rubbed it in her hair. Within seconds, her hair looked disgusting. It hung in long greasy strings.

"Gross," Becka commented.

"That's the idea," Cat replied. Then she examined her scrubbed, makeupless face in the mirror. "Good," she said. "I look like death warmed over." Becka didn't think Cat looked at all bad, except for the hair, of course, but she didn't argue.

Becka continued to watch as Cat rummaged through Josie's dresser drawer.

"Aha! These are perfect!" Cat held up one of Josie's most disreputable pants. They were faded, worn, and had spots and stains. She stripped off her immaculate jeans and put Josie's pants on. They were a little big around the waist, so they hung down almost to her hips. And they were at least a couple inches too short.

"That looks awful!" Becka exclaimed.

"Good." Cat then went to her own drawer, rummaged around, and pulled out an old flowered shirt. It had been pretty once, but was now too small and too tight. It also had a rip at the shoulder. Cat put it on.

"What do you think?"

Becka was practically speechless. "I don't know. You sure don't look like you. I can't figure out—"

"Honestly, Becka, for someone who's read so much, you can be really dense. I'm going to explain it to you one more time. If the Morgans want to adopt me, it's because they like me the way I am, right? What they're going to see today is the opposite of me. So they won't want to adopt me. Now do you get it?"

"I got it before, Cat. What I can't figure out is how *I* should act."

"Well, they probably don't want to adopt you anyway. But just in case, don't bring any books."

"Where's Cat?" Josie asked. She and Becka were on the steps waiting for the Morgans.

"Upstairs. She doesn't want to come down till they get here." Becka giggled nervously. "I think she's afraid of anyone here seeing her. It would ruin her reputation."

"How does she think *I* feel?" Josie grumbled. She tugged at the short, hot-pink skirt Cat had loaned her.

110

"You look okay," Becka said. "Not like you, but okay."

"Thanks a lot." Josie pulled the skirt down again. It was uncomfortable. And the stupid barrettes in her hair were giving her a headache. She had known she'd hate dressing like this, but Cat had insisted that Josie do her part.

She looked at Becka's faded peasant dress with annoyance. "How come you get to wear your regular clothes?"

"Because nothing you guys have would fit me."

Josie gazed off into the distance. "Here they come."

Becka ran back into Willoughby Hall, and Josie heard her yelling for Cat. She clutched the foil-covered plate in her hand and headed toward the driveway as the blue station wagon pulled in.

"Josie, hi," Annie called from the car window. She was smiling, but Josie could see her forehead pucker as she took in Josie's appearance.

That was nothing compared to her expression when she saw Cat. But neither she nor Ben remarked on it as the three girls piled into the back seat. *Too polite,* Josie thought.

"It's great to see you all again," Ben said as he steered the car out onto the road. Becka smiled and opened her mouth, but Cat elbowed her in the ribs. Becka's mouth snapped shut.

"So, what have you girls been up to?" Annie

asked. She turned around in her seat and smiled. None of the girls looked at her.

"Not much," Cat replied. She looked out the window and bit her nails in a bored fashion.

"The usual," Josie said, and yawned. Out of the corner of her eye she could see Annie quickly look at Ben. Josie hardened herself to follow through with their plan. It was the only way.

Ben looked back at them through the rearview mirror. "Becka, how's *David Copperfield* going? I'll bet you finished it already."

Becka bit her trembling lip. "No. I don't think I will. It's kind of boring. And there's not enough sex."

Cat stifled a gasp, but she could hear Annie's quickly drawn breath. *Where had Becka come up with that?* Cat wondered admiringly. It was brilliant!

Josie couldn't see Ben's reaction, but she could imagine it. The Morgans sure weren't getting what they bargained for! She sneaked a peek at Becka and saw that she was staring hard out the window. Josie knew it was difficult for Becka to lie like that.

Annie tried again. "What's that in your lap?" she asked Josie.

"Brownies," Josie replied.

"Great!" Ben said. Josie felt almost sick. He wouldn't think it was so great later.

The park was just a few minutes away. Ben, his guitar hanging over his shoulder, carried the hamper to a wooded spot near a stream. "Isn't this the perfect place for a picnic?" Annie asked.

112

Cat grunted in reply.

"If you like that kind of thing," Josie said.

"I thought you loved the outdoors," Ben said as he spread a thick plaid blanket on the grass.

Josie just shrugged. "Too many bugs," she said. "They're icky." She tried to sit down, but it wasn't easy, wearing Cat's awful little skirt. Finally she just dropped, hands firmly holding down the sides.

"It's chilly here," Becka complained. Annie looked in bewilderment at the hot sun blazing down. "Um, I think we have a sweater in the car," she began uncertainly.

"Then it would be too hot," Becka said, and frowned down at the ground. Ben looked at Annie, his eyebrows raised.

"Well, maybe we should eat," Annie said.

"That's a good idea!" Ben said cheerfully. He turned to the girls. "Annie has been planning this picnic for days." When no one reacted, Annie opened the hamper and began to take food out.

"We've got chicken salad sandwiches here."

"Ugh," Cat said. "I hate chicken salad."

"I'll take two," Becka said. Annie's eyes widened, but she put two sandwiches on a paper plate and handed them to Becka. Becka started eating one, but Josie could tell her heart wasn't in it.

"I'm not hungry," Josie said. It was true. She felt like she would choke if she tried to eat anything. "And anyway," she added, "I'm watching my figure."

"There's tuna, too," Annie said. When no one responded to her offer, Annie looked sad. For a fleeting moment, Cat couldn't help feeling sorry for her. But she wasn't going to back down now.

"I don't like tuna any better than chicken," she said, and she flopped down on the grass. She lay flat on her back and covered her eyes with her arm.

"I'm going to take a nap. Wake me when this is over," she said. Annie and Ben looked at each other again. Ben shrugged.

"There's fresh fruit, too," he said.

"Too messy," Josie declared. "I don't want to get my hands sticky."

"I'll take two tuna sandwiches, too," Becka said. Underneath the shadow of her arm, Cat almost smiled. Becka was really going above and beyond the call of duty!

"She eats everything in sight," Josie informed Ben and Annie. "We have to hide all the food in the kitchen."

No one made any more conversation, but Ben and Annie each tried to eat a sandwich. Josie watched as Becka determinedly started on her second chicken salad. She hoped Becka wouldn't make herself sick. On the other hand, *that* really would convince Ben and Annie!

"That was delicious, honey," Ben said firmly as he finished his sandwich. Annie nodded weakly. "Now for some dessert! Pass me those terrific brownies," he said.

Josie averted her eyes. She couldn't bear to look as

Ben bit into his brownie. She couldn't cover her ears, though. As he coughed and sputtered, she cringed inside.

"What is it, Ben?" Annie asked anxiously. She poured some lemonade from the thermos into a paper cup. Ben practically snatched it from her and gulped it down.

When he recovered, he stared at the remainder of the brownie in his hand. "Uh, Josie, these aren't like the ones you made at our house."

"They're not?" Josie asked innocently. She took one, turned her head, and pretended to take a bite. "Gosh. I must have used salt instead of sugar."

"Well, anyone can make a mistake," Annie said.

"Yeah. I'm just not interested in cooking anymore."

"What about horses?" Annie asked softly.

Josie picked up a blade of grass and carefully tore it. "Nah. I lost my interest in them, too."

Cat sat up. "Josie's like that. Very unpredictable. One day she likes something, the next day, she hates it. We think maybe she has a split personality."

This is too much, Josie thought.

She didn't want the Morgans to *hate* her. "Wait a minute," she broke in. "I'm not *that* crazy."

Cat's eyes practically burned a hole in her.

"Yes, you are," she said.

Ben looked from Cat to Josie. "She's not the only one who's unpredictable."

"Oh, this is the real me," Cat assured him. "I'm just a natural slob."

"We have to beg her to take a bath sometimes," Becka agreed.

"We've got her up to twice a week," Josie added cheerfully.

Ben scratched his head. "Becka, I'm sorry you didn't like *David Copperfield*. What else have you been reading?"

"Nothing," Becka said. "I really don't like to read."

"But you said . . . wait a minute. Do you have a split personality, too?"

"No," Cat said quickly. "She just lies a lot."

"And steals," Josie put in quickly.

Annie and Ben exchanged looks again. "Well," Ben said finally, "how about a sing-along?" He took his guitar and began strumming. "Everyone knows this one. 'I've been working on the railroad . . .' "

Annie joined in. " 'All the livelong day. I've been working on the railroad, just to pass the time . . .' " Their voices trailed off when they realized none of the girls was singing along.

"I guess no one feels like singing," Annie said. "How about playing Scrabble? I brought a game with me."

"I'm not up for a game," Cat said.

"Me neither," Josie echoed. Becka just shook her head.

"What would you like to do then?" Ben asked.

The girls eyed each other. Then Cat spoke. "Go home. Back to Willoughby Hall."

Ben and Annie were staring at them as if all three of the girls were complete strangers. Which, in a way, they were.

"All right," Annie said quietly. "Let's go."

They picked everything up and went back to the car. Then they drove back in complete silence.

Ellen was in the entrance hall when they returned. "You're back early!"

"The girls wanted to return," Ben said. "And we'd like to see Mrs. Scanlon."

Becka shot a worried look at the others. The Morgans were going to report their behavior. How many demerits would that mean? Probably a million.

"Mrs. Scanlon's usually very busy," Cat said. "You shouldn't bother her."

"Cat!" Ellen exclaimed. "I'm sure Mrs. Scanlon would be delighted to see the Morgans."

"Want to bet?" Josie muttered.

Ellen's mouth fell open. "Josie!"

"May we go in?" Annie asked.

"Of course," Ellen replied. "Girls, aren't you going to thank the Morgans?"

All three had their eyes glued to the floor. None spoke. "I'm very sorry," Ellen started to say, but Ben held up his hand.

"That's all right. We'll go see Mrs. Scanlon," he said. They went down the hall.

Ellen turned to the girls. "What are you guys doing? You were acting horribly! Don't you want to be adopted?"

"No," Becka murmured.

"Why?"

Becka and Josie looked at Cat. "We have to stay together," Cat said. "We're a team. We don't want to be separated."

Becka thought it was fortunate Ellen hadn't been at Willoughby Hall very long. She actually seemed to believe Cat.

"Oh. I see." She studied the girls for a moment. "You three better hang around. Mrs. Scanlon might want to talk to you." She turned and headed down to the director's office.

"What's the matter with you?" Cat asked Becka. "You look like you're about to burst into tears."

"I don't know. I just feel sort of depressed."

"Why? The plan worked. I feel great."

"Really?" Cat didn't look so great to Becka, and it wasn't just because of her appearance. Her eyes had a strange, glazed look.

"We'll probably get demerits," Josie said.

"So what?" Cat said. "That's not the end of the world. And what we did is worth a few demerits. Isn't it?"

No one answered her.

"I feel stupid just standing here," Josie said. "Let's go into the TV room."

Becka hoped the room would be empty, but Trixie

was in there. She eyed them with interest. "What happened?"

"None of your business," Cat said.

"Oh, I get it," Trixie said. "They decided they don't want any of you."

Josie slumped down into the sofa. "Yeah, that's right. Why don't you run over to Mrs. Scanlon's office? They're still here. Maybe they'll take you."

Trixie scowled. "How many times do I have to tell you? I've *got* parents!"

"Oh, knock it off," Cat muttered. "You're making that up."

"I am not!"

"Oh yeah?" Cat glared at her. "Then what are you doing in an orphanage?"

Trixie jumped up. "It's none of your business! And anyway, I'm going back to my parents in a year."

Becka eyed her sadly. "Trixie, you shouldn't lie to yourself like that."

"I'm not lying!"

"Then where are your parents?" Cat challenged her. "Tell us!"

Trixie's eyes were blazing. "Okay, I will! They're in jail! Are you satisfied?" She ran out of the room.

The girls stared after her. "Wow," Becka breathed. "In jail. Poor kid. No wonder she didn't want anyone to know."

Cat shuddered. "Imagine having parents who are prisoners. I'd die of embarrassment. That's worse than being an orphan."

119

"I'm not so sure about that," Josie said. "At least she knows she'll get out of here in a year."

Becka chewed on a fingernail. "Ben and Annie would never do anything that could get them sent to jail."

Cat looked at her sharply. "What's *that* supposed to mean?"

"Nothing," Becka said quickly.

They all lapsed into silence. Furtively, Becka took a sidelong glance at Josie and Cat. Were they thinking what she was thinking? That maybe—just, maybe—they'd blown a major chance for one of them?

The door opened and Mrs. Scanlon walked in, followed by the Morgans. To Becka's surprise, none of them seemed terribly angry.

"The Morgans told me about the picnic," Mrs. Scanlon said. "At first, I was very upset with you girls. But then Ellen came in and told us how you felt." She eyed the girls curiously. "I never realized you felt so close to each other."

Becka detected a twinkle in her eye. Mrs. Scanlon had to know that was a big lie. She'd seen how they were together.

Cat spoke up. "I know we don't act like such good friends all the time." Her tone had that sweet, phony sound Becka and Josie knew well. "But we're really a team. We're like the Three—what are they called?"

"Musketeers," Becka murmured.

"Yes, like the Three Musketeers."

"We understand," Ben said. "We figured that's

120

why you were all acting so strangely today. You hoped we wouldn't adopt one of you, because you don't want to be separated."

"And you won't have to be," Annie said. "It's all going to work out. You see . . ." She paused. "You tell them, Ben."

Ben smiled. "We'd decided even before we came here today. We want to adopt all three of you."

Becka stood very still. Was she dreaming? Could this be real? Was she really being adopted, going home with a real family? She felt fuzzy and warm, like her whole body was glowing.

She looked at the others. They looked just as dazed as she felt.

"Isn't this wonderful, girls?" Mrs. Scanlon said. "Now you *will* be sisters. You'll never be separated. You'll be together forever."

Sisters. Together forever. As the words sunk in, Becka felt that warm glow start to fade.

She didn't have to look at the others to know they were feeling exactly the same.

Ten

Three days later, Cat was searching under her bed for anything she might have left there. She discovered a pair of sunglasses. She crawled back out, got up, tossed them into a box, and grimaced.

"This is so embarrassing, having to carry our stuff to the Morgans in cardboard boxes."

Josie was sitting on the floor in front of the dresser. "I don't think they expect orphans to have matching sets of luggage."

"We're not orphans anymore," Becka reminded her. She was sitting by the little bookcase. She couldn't resist opening each book and reading a page or two before carefully placing it in the box beside her.

Cat went to the closet, which was practically

empty. "I'm not taking that old winter coat. Annie and Ben can buy me a new one."

"Hey, Cat, they're not rich," Josie said.

"Not now," Cat said. "But they could be. I mean, they could expand that health-food store. Maybe even end up with a whole chain of stores." The notion pleased her. She envisioned Morgan's Country Foods at every mall all over the country.

Josie eyed Becka sternly. "You haven't cleared out half that bookcase. Are you planning to read each book over before you pack it?"

Becka hastily closed the book in her lap. "No. I was just thinking." She smiled happily. "It's going to be so neat to say things like, 'My mother gave me this,' or 'My father's going to pick me up.'"

Mother. Father. Josie looked at the brown envelope in her hand. She turned furtively to make sure the others weren't looking. Then she sneaked a peek inside.

Her real mother and father were smiling in the old photographs. Josie had a feeling they were smiling at her right this minute. They were happy for her. "You'd like them," she whispered.

"What did you say?" Cat asked.

"Nothing." Josie closed the envelope and placed it in her box.

"I still can't believe they're adopting all three of us," Becka said in a dreamy voice.

"Only because we told them we had to stay together," Cat replied. "Me and my brilliant ideas."

123

"That's not true," Josie objected. "You heard what Ben said. They'd decided they wanted all of us even before they heard that."

Becka turned to Josie with an anxious expression. "And I believed him. I think they really do want us all. Don't you think so?"

Josie got up. "I'll be back in a few minutes." She had to get out of there. Becka's question had stirred the fears she'd almost managed to bury.

She hurried downstairs and went to the kitchen.

"I was wondering if you were going to say good-bye," Mrs. Parker said, smiling. Josie allowed herself to be engulfed in a hug.

"What if it doesn't work out?" she asked. "What if I don't like it there? What if they hate me?"

She wasn't sure the cook could hear her, her voice was so muffled. But apparently she could. Or she'd read her mind. Mrs. Parker released her and held her at arm's length. "Listen to me, Josie. Life is full of 'what ifs.' You're going to have to take some chances." Her face softened. "Besides, you know you'll always have a home here."

How could she leave her? Josie wondered. How could she leave the one place where she knew for sure that one person loved her?

She was horrified to realize she was on the verge of tears. "I'll visit," she managed to say.

"Of course you will," Mrs. Parker said briskly. "Now, your new parents are going to be here any minute. Have you finished packing?"

"No," Josie admitted.

"Then get along with you."

Josie looked at her closely. Were those tears in Mrs. Parker's eyes? Impulsively, she moved closer and kissed the cook's cheek. Then she turned and ran out.

She almost collided with Trixie on the staircase. "Trixie, hi."

"Hi," Trixie mumbled.

"Listen, I'm sorry about the other day. When Cat was teasing you about your parents."

Trixie shrugged. "It's okay. Everyone is bound to find out sooner or later. In case you're wondering, they're in jail because of some tax thing. It's not like they robbed a bank or anything."

Her woebegone face touched Josie. "Hey, you want to come up to our room? We're just packing up."

"Okay."

"What's *she* doing here?" Cat asked as they walked in.

"I invited her. I can have friends in my room if I want," Josie said.

Cat made a face. "I hope we're each going to have our own room at the Morgans'."

"Why don't you ask them when they get here?" Josie suggested. "If they say we have to share, you can always say you changed your mind and want to stay here. That would be okay with me."

Cat glared at her. She picked up her blow dryer and put it in Becka's box.

"Hey!" Becka cried. "What do you think you're doing?"

"I don't have any room left in my box."

"But I've still got more books to put in there!"

"What's more important? Your books or my hair dryer?"

"My books."

"That's a matter of opinion," Cat shot back.

Trixie was observing this in fascination. "Wow. This is going to be weird."

"What do you mean?" Josie asked.

"How are you three going to live together in the same house?"

"We've been living together here," Josie pointed out.

"Yeah, but that's different," Trixie said. "Here you're just roommates. Now you're going to be a *family.*"

The room became very still.

"We'll manage," Josie said.

"Yeah," Cat added. Becka nodded. But the looks Trixie saw on their faces didn't exactly suggest sisterly love.

There was a knock on the door, and Mrs. Scanlon walked in. "Are you girls ready?"

There was a flurry of last-minute running around. Mrs. Scanlon strolled through the room, looking

126

around and checking drawers. She paused when she reached the closet. "There's a coat in here."

"It's mine," Cat said. "I'm leaving it. I figure they'll buy me a new one."

Mrs. Scanlon took the coat out of the closet. "Cat, I wouldn't expect too much if I were you. Remember, the Morgans are going to have *three* daughters! You're not going to be able to have everything you want."

Cat watched in dismay as she folded the coat and placed it in a box. Well, Mrs. Scanlon didn't know everything, she thought. All Cat had to do was to become the favorite daughter. Then they'd buy her anything she wanted. And somehow she'd do that—become their favorite.

The boys arrived, and everyone began lugging boxes downstairs. It seemed like half the orphanage's population was in the entrance hall. The next few minutes were taken up with hugs and kisses.

Becka felt a hand tugging on her skirt. She looked down at one of the younger kids. "Who's going to read to us?" he asked.

Gazing down at his wistful face, Becka felt waves of sadness pass over her. She was going to miss the little ones. She was going to miss everything and everybody.

Suddenly she was very frightened. What was she doing, going off into the unknown like this? Okay, she'd had plenty of fantasies about being adopted. But fantasies were dreams she could plan and control.

This was real life. This was happening. She couldn't control it.

Her thoughts raced wildly. It wasn't too late. She could still back out.

Just then the front door opened. Annie and Ben walked in. There was a whirl of final good-byes, calls of "good luck" and "be good." Feeling dazed, Becka soon found herself sitting in the back seat of the clunky blue station wagon along with Josie and Cat. Turning, she could see Ben and Annie putting their boxes in the back.

"Move over," Cat said to Josie. "You're crushing me."

"I can't," Josie said. "There's no room."

"Then you move, Becka."

"There's no place to move," Becka replied. "What do you want me to do, hang out the window?"

"But my dress is getting crushed," Cat complained.

"Too bad," Josie replied.

Then Cat noticed something. "Becka, is that my gold barrette in your hair?"

"Yeah, I borrowed it."

"You should have asked first!"

"What's the big deal? I'll give it back to you."

"Shh," Josie hissed. "They're coming."

The car doors opened and Ben and Annie got in. Ben started the engine. Annie turned around and gazed at the girls. "I'm so happy," she said simply.

"Why did you decide to take all three of us?" Josie blurted out.

"Because you're each so unique," Annie replied. "And yet you each seem so right for us."

Watching the road, Ben nodded. "The way we figured it, if we're going to have one daughter, we might as well have three."

"And besides," Annie continued, "if we only adopted one of you, you'd be an only child. Now you've got sisters."

Sisters. That word again. Josie shifted uneasily.

"And you can stay a team, just like you've always been," Ben added.

Some team, Cat thought. If only they knew.

"We're going to be great," Ben continued happily. "One big happy family."

Becka gave the others a sidelong look and wondered if they were thinking what she was thinking. Big, yes. Happy?

Well, if they had gotten this far, anything was possible. Her spirits lifted as she watched the road unwinding before her. And, like the others, she wondered what lay ahead.

Here's a sneak peek at what's ahead in the exciting second book of THREE OF A KIND: *Home's a Nice Place to Visit, But I Wouldn't Want to Live There.*

The doors of the County courthouse swung open, and out stepped a brand-new family—Ben and Annie Morgan and their new daughters, Becka, Cat, and Josie.

"Becka? Are you all right?" Annie Morgan asked.

Becka turned and smiled. "I'm fine, Annie. Better than fine." She wished she could think of the right word to describe how she was feeling. *Wonderful, fabulous, fantastic . . .* She took a deep breath of fresh air. "I'm Becka Morgan today," she said dreamily.

Cat rolled her eyes. "Brilliant," she drawled. "She knows her own name."

"And how do you like yours?" Ben asked Becka's new sister.

Cat pronounced her name slowly. "Cat Morgan.

131

Catherine Morgan. I like it! Don't you think it sounds even more glamorous than Cat O'Grady?"

Annie put her arm around Cat's shoulders and gave them a quick squeeze. "I think it sounds like the name of my daughter," she said warmly. Annie turned to Josie, whose hands were thrust deeply into the pockets of her skirt. "And you're Josie Morgan."

"Josie *Taylor* Morgan," Josie corrected her.

"Of course," Annie said quickly. "And a beautiful name it is."

"But Morgan really isn't our name yet, is it?" Josie asked.

"Well, no, not legally," Ben said. "Those were the preliminary adoption papers we just signed. We'll be signing the final ones in a few weeks."

Cat grinned, showing the dimples in her smooth cheeks. "Does that mean we're all just here on approval?"

"You got it, kid. One false move and you're out of here," Ben said, pretending to look fierce.

Becka laughed, but she couldn't help feeling a prickle of apprehension. She knew Ben was just teasing, but even so, it was awful to think her new parents could change their minds—could actually send them back to the orphanage. They wouldn't do that, Becka assured herself. Not in a million years. But still, they *could.*

"Come on, let's go home," Annie said, starting down the wide courthouse steps between Ben and Cat.

"I love hearing her say that," Becka said. " 'Let's go home.' Doesn't it sound wonderful?"

It was a short drive to the Morgans' weathered gray farmhouse. It was a huge, slightly ramshackle place that Ben was slowly renovating one room at a time. Becka watched Cat's upper lip curl as the battered blue station wagon pulled into the gravel driveway. She knew that Cat would much prefer to be living in a fancy mansion.

As far as Becka was concerned, the house was just fine—cozy and comfortable, the way a *home* should be.

Everyone got out and went up the front stairs, automatically avoiding the broken step. Inside, Annie headed directly toward the kitchen. "I'm going to get lunch started."

"Would you like some help?" Becka asked.

"No, thanks," Annie called over her shoulder. "This is your special day, girls. No chores."

"Sounds good to me," Cat said cheerfully.

Becka looked at her pointedly. "We could set the table," she persisted.

Ben tousled Becka's hair. "All you're responsible for is getting washed up. And you can change into something more comfortable if you like."

Becka felt Cat's hand on her back, shoving her toward the stairs. She allowed herself to be pushed along, and Josie followed silently.

Halfway up the stairs, out of Ben's earshot, Cat hissed, "Quit offering to help like that. They might take us up on it!"

"It wouldn't kill you to volunteer once in a while," Becka fired back. She turned to Josie, who was dragging herself up the stairs. "Josie, why don't you help Annie in the kitchen? You like to cook. You used to help Mrs. Parker back at Willoughby Hall all the time."

"It's not the same here," Josie said, passing Becka and glumly opening their bedroom door. Within seconds she'd removed the skirt and blouse she had worn to the courthouse and was back in her usual beat-up jeans and T-shirt.

Their bedroom was large, bigger than the one they had shared at Willoughby Hall. There were three beds, three dressers, and one large closet.

"Cat, you didn't make your bed," Becka pointed out. "And your nightgown's still on the floor."

"So what?" Cat said, flopping down on her bed.

Becka frowned. "You're going to wrinkle your dress."

"Quit nagging," Cat replied. She stretched out and wiggled around in a deliberate attempt to wrinkle the dress even more. "Besides, Annie will iron it."

She was right. Since they had moved here, Annie had been knocking herself out doing things for them. But still, Cat's attitude annoyed Becka. "Annie's not your personal maid, you know. She's our mother," Becka said.

"No, she isn't," Josie said.

Becka looked at her in surprise. "What do you mean? Okay, maybe she's not our official mother yet,

134

but she will be. If we get through this trial period."
Becka set her lips together. Nothing was going to
stop her from finally having a family of her own, forever.

She went over to her dresser and pulled out some
baggy shorts and a T-shirt. Then she crossed to Cat's
bed, picked up the nightgown off the floor, and began
folding it neatly. Cat stared at her. "What are you
doing? Trying out for a gold medal? The 'best daughter' award? Honestly, Becka, you're being such a
goody-goody."

"Well, I'd rather be a goody-goody than a selfish,
greedy ingrate!"

Cat looked shocked. Becka hardly ever got really
angry. "Oh, shut up," Cat shouted.

"You shut up!"

Josie whirled around. "Both of you shut up!"

Becka bit her lip. Josie was right. The last thing
she wanted was for Ben and Annie to hear them argu-
ing. "I'm going downstairs," she said and marched
out, with Josie following her. Cat stood in front of the
mirror, brushing her hair.

When the family was gathered around the lunch
table, Becka's eyes darted back and forth between Cat
and Josie. Annie didn't appear to notice anything
wrong while she served lunch. Becka began to eat the
salad that Annie had made, her mind clouded by all
she had to think about.

Sisters, ha. Some sisters. They were supposed to
love each other. Instead it was as if she and Cat were

rivals on opposing teams. And Josie was playing a whole other game of her own somewhere. But if three loving sisters were what Annie and Ben wanted, that's what they would get, Becka promised herself grimly. Becka was determined: From today on, she and Josie and Cat would be best friends—no matter how much they hated one another.